# THE SOLAIRE TRILOGY

## THOMAS FINCHAM

**The Solaire Trilogy**
Thomas Fincham



**AUTHOR'S NOTE**

This book is a work of fiction. Names, characters, places and incidents are products of the author's imagination or are used fictitiously. Any resemblance to actual events or locales or persons, living or dead, is entirely coincidental.

Visit the author's website:
**www.finchambooks.com**

Contact:
**finchambooks@gmail.com**

Join my Facebook page:
**https://www.facebook.com/finchambooks/**

# A SPY THRILLER

# TABLE OF CONTENTS

# FOREWORD

**Dear Reader,**

**Thank you for checking out my work.**

**As a child, I grew up watching James Bond movies with my dad, and when I got older, I read some of Ian Fleming's original work. Inspired by the character and the writing, I tried to create my version of a secret agent. *The Solaire Trilogy* is my feeble attempt at the spy genre. It's a collection of three novellas in one book.**

**I hope you enjoy reading it.**

**Sincerely,**
**Thomas Fincham**

## The Crystal Towers

THE HAGUE

"This is not good," the first man said. He had an English accent.

The other man did not reply but understood.

They were in a room, staring out at the old cobblestone street below.

"The international community is keeping a close eye on us. Unless we make solid progress, we will be deemed irrelevant," the Englishman said.

The other man shook his head and said in a Dutch accent, "The mission in New York was a total failure."

"It doesn't have to be," said a voice from the other end of the room.

They both turned. They'd forgotten he was still there.

The Englishman said incredulously, "The agent was found shot fourteen times. It was a complete disaster and a foolish mistake."

"The mistake was that you sent an agent. We were lucky it didn't lead back to us. We have to send someone else."

"Another agent?" the Englishman asked.

"No. No more agents or spies."

The Dutchman asked, "Then who?"

The man smiled. "I have someone in mind."

TORONTO

The heavyset man was sucking down spaghetti like it was his last meal. Sauce covered his lips and chin. He grunted as he inhaled more noodles.

Behind him, two burly men merely sipped water. Unbeknownst to the patrons of the restaurant, the two men were bodyguards for the spaghetti-loving gourmand, and they each packed automatic pistols.

A waiter approached the man. "Is everything to your liking, sir?"

"Yeah," the heavyset man replied. "Get me another plate."

"Of course, sir."

The waiter soon reappeared with another plate of spaghetti.

"Sir, if you don't mind me saying, you have something on your chin."

The two bodyguards gave the waiter a hard look.

The heavyset man touched his chin and then turned to his bodyguards. "At least someone's got the balls to tell me I look disgusting."

Neither of his two bodyguards said a word.

"Sir," the waiter said. "You would be more comfortable if you took off your jacket. Allow me to assist you."

The waiter went around and proceeded to remove the heavyset man's jacket, which he then placed on the man's chair.

The waiter snapped his wrist and, as if by magic, out came a cloth napkin. "Sir."

The heavyset man turned to his bodyguards. "Now that's what I call service."

The heavyset man loosened his tie, unbuttoned his shirt collar, and allowed the waiter to place the napkin firmly on his lap.

"Is there anything else I can do for you?" the waiter asked with a slight bow.

"No, that's fine. I'll make sure you get a good tip."

"You're very kind."

The heavyset man resumed gorging on his meal.

The waiter disappeared into the back.

Instead of returning, the waiter moved past the kitchen and emerged from the back of the restaurant.

"Thanks, Luigi," he said, handing the restaurant's owner a few bills.

He got on a 1974 BMW motorcycle and rode off.

***

Two hours later, the motorcycle rider turned into a back alley. He parked the bike behind a dilapidated house. He didn't bother locking up the bike. There was no need; it was beat-up and rusted through and through. If anyone did steal it, they'd be doing him a favor.

He headed down the steps to the basement.

When he entered and turned the lights on, he froze.

A man was sitting on his sofa.

The man was wearing a beige overcoat. His hands were in his pockets, and his eyes were fixed on him.

"Please, come and sit down," the man said.

He thought about turning and running back up the stairs, but at the angle the man was sitting, he'd have no problem firing shots and hitting him.

He wasn't going to risk it if the man did indeed have a gun.

He sat across from him.

The man pulled his hands from his pockets and placed them in front of himself.

The man said, "Mr. Bind… Jim Bind, isn't it?"

"Yes," Bind slowly said.

"It's a nice place you have here."

The man looked around the basement apartment. It was cramped, to say the least. There was a small kitchen that could fit only one person at a time. Beside the kitchen was a bathroom with a standing shower, and next to that, a bedroom with a mattress on the floor.

"What do you want?" Bind finally asked him.

"I'll tell you in a minute," the man replied, "but first, what you did at the restaurant was impressive."

This took Bind aback.

The man smiled. "I was there. I was impressed by how you managed to pull off the fat man's neck chain without him or his bodyguards realizing it."

From his pocket, Bind removed a silver string with a key on it. "How did you know?"

"I've been watching you. For the past three months, you have been *working* at that restaurant, and I'm using the word *working* very kindly. You've been observing the fat man, monitoring his every movement. What time he came in, what he ordered, and who he was with. It was today that you made your move—a very ingenious one, if I may say so.

But I have a question: how did you know where the key was?"

"Whenever he sat down and got up, he touched his chest."

"Won't he realize it's missing when he touches his chest and doesn't feel it tonight?"

"I switched it."

The man raised an eyebrow. *"Impressive."* The man removed a letter-size brown envelope and placed it in front of him.

"What is it?" Bind asked.

"Take a look."

He did. Inside were four black and white photos. One showed Bind on his motorcycle in front of a building, another of him entering a room, another of him coming out of it, and the last was of him leaving the building.

"How much did you find?" the man asked.

Bind didn't know how to answer.

"Okay," the man said. "This is what I know, and you can fill in the rest. The fat man's name is Georgio Draggone, a local thug. He's been threatening local shopkeepers. In return for their safety, they pay him to leave them alone. It is known that Georgio owes money to some very dangerous people, so he has intensified his visits to these shopkeepers. They, in turn, hired you to find something to get rid of him. You did." The man crossed his legs. "In your possession, you have Draggone's entire monetary collection. I'm guessing over fifty thousand dollars."

Bind said nothing.

"What I'm interested in is what you are going to do with it," the man said.

"What do you mean?"

"You know exactly what I mean. Are you going to keep the entire amount, or are you going to give it back to the shopkeepers?"

"I'm going to keep it."

The man laughed hard. "Why is it that I don't believe you?"

"It's a lot of money, so why wouldn't I?"

"You've done these… *assignments* many times before," the man said. "And if you do keep the money, then why do you live in squalor?"

Bind looked around his apartment. "It's temporary."

"I'm sure it is."

Bind's face tightened. "This is the last time I'm going to ask you. What do you want?"

The man removed a card and dropped it on the table in front of him. "Tomorrow, I want you to meet me at this place."

Without looking at the card, Bind said, "Why should I?"

"Because I have these," the man said, pointing to the photos. "And you wouldn't want them in the hands of the police, would you?"

Bind said, "They don't show anything."

"Oh, we have more, many more," the man said. "Believe me."

Bind said nothing.

The man got up and headed for the door. He stopped and turned. "One more thing. I don't like the name *Jim Bind*. It is so dull and boring. I do like your real name, though. It sounds so much more interesting. *Mr. Roman Solaire.*"

With that, the man was gone.

***

Roman Solaire went to the Art Gallery of Ontario in downtown Toronto. He went in through the front entrance, purchased his ticket, and went straight to level one. He turned left and entered the Thomson Collection.

Inside the vault-like gallery, he found the man. He was standing in front of a large painting.

Solaire joined him.

"It is called *The Massacre of the Innocents*, painted by Peter Paul Rubens in 1612," the man said. "There is a second version in Munich." He turned to Solaire. "Do you know how much it is worth? Over a hundred million dollars."

Solaire didn't seem impressed.

The man said, "I know you're not here to talk about art."

They moved to a corner of the gallery.

From his coat, the man pulled out a folder and held it for Solaire.

He did not take it. Instead, he said, "Your name?"

"Call me, Mr. Travers, if you like."

Solaire eyed him.

The man smiled. "That's all you'll get for now."

Solaire took the folder.

Inside was a photo of a man coming out of a black vehicle. The man's head was clean-shaven, he was of slight build, and he wore an expensive suit.

"His name is Guy Fox. Have you heard of him?" the man asked.

Solaire shook his head.

"Fox is a real estate developer in New York. He is worth a lot of money."

Solaire looked up from the folder. "If you want me to steal money, I won't do it."

"Not money… evidence."

"Evidence?"

Travers pulled out another photo. In this one, Fox was standing beside an African-looking man.

"This was taken in the Congo. We believe Fox is sponsoring state terrorism in Africa. We have several more photos of him with other unsavory characters."

"What do you want me to do about it?" Solaire asked.

"We want you to find evidence that links him to these people."

"What about the photos? Why not use them?"

"Circumstantial. We need something that can hold up in court."

Solaire didn't know what to say.

"Fox is having the grand opening of his new venture, Crystal Towers, in New York City. We want you to go there and find the evidence we need."

"You're not even telling me what exactly I'm looking for."

"If we knew, Mr. Solaire, then we wouldn't need you."

"Why should I do it?"

"We have *your* photos."

"That's blackmail."

"Let's call it incentive."

Solaire thought for a moment. "You want me to go to New York?"

Travers pulled out another envelope from his coat.

Solaire was tempted to ask Travers how many pockets he had in that coat of his, but he decided against it.

Inside the envelope was a bundle of hundred-dollar bills, a US passport, and a plane ticket to New York.

"Who do you work for?" Solaire asked, examining the passport. It contained his name and photo.

"Let's say we can get things expedited. Will you do it?"

"Do I have a choice?"

"I would love to say yes, but we need your help."

Solaire felt the US bills. "It's a lot of money."

"There's more if you need it."

Solaire stuffed the envelope in his pocket.

"One more thing," Travers said. He held out a cell phone. "It's secure. Only I have the number. You answer it when I call."

"If I don't?"

"Then, I'll consider you dead."

Solaire took the phone. It was a bulky, older model, but it looked solid.

Travers moved away from him.

"One last thing," he said. "I would do with a change of wardrobe."

Solaire looked down at his battered jeans, scuffed boots, and faded shirt.

Travers disappeared into an adjacent room.

Solaire looked back at *The Massacre of the Innocents*.

He felt like *he* was walking into a massacre.

NEW YORK

American Airlines flight 3826 landed at JFK International Airport and taxied to Terminal 8. After disembarking the plane, Roman Solaire headed for the US citizens line. The line was long, but it was moving fast.

Solaire was pulling his sole luggage: a carry-on. He didn't pack heavy, so there was no need to worry about baggage claim. But that was not what he was concerned about; it was the small blue book in his hand with the words *United States of America* engraved in silver on its cover.

The last two days had been surreal. First meeting Travers, and now attempting to enter the United States with false documentation. He had spent a great deal of time examining the passport in detail, but he could find no indication that it was forged. The document looked like the real deal.

*Who is this Travers?* he thought. *And what agency does he work for?*

His turn came. He approached the counter, where a heavyset female officer examined his passport. She looked at the photo and then at him. Looking satisfied, she stamped the passport and said, "Welcome home, sir."

"Thank you," Solaire said.

He quickly left the terminal.

Outside, the air was cool.

He glanced around and found a taxi stand. His driver, a man wearing a turban, placed his carry-on in the trunk.

The driver said his name was Jagjit Singh, or Jag, as his friends called him.

Solaire inquired about the best hotels in New York.

Jag rattled off names like the Pierre, Mandarin Oriental, the Plaza, and the Ritz-Carlton.

Solaire asked him where *he* would prefer to stay.

"Ritz-Carlton for me," Jag replied.

"Then that's where I'll be staying," Solaire said.

The ride was forty-five minutes, during which time Solaire kept his eyes closed.

He wasn't sure what he was doing here, but a part of him knew he had no choice.

Travers seemed like a man who knew what he wanted and how to get it. Plus, Solaire was intrigued by this whole "assignment," if one could call it that.

The taxi stopped in front of a white building.

Solaire paid his fare and generously tipped Jag.

"I'll be leaving in a couple of days," Solaire said. "Why don't you come by and drive me back to the airport?"

"Yes, sir!" Jag said, counting the extra cash.

***

Solaire rented the Deluxe Room, located on the fourteenth floor of the hotel. The room had a king-size bed, interior view of the courtyard, a Sony flat-screen TV with a DVD player, two chairs, and a writing desk.

Solaire wasn't sure that he'd use the writing desk, so he placed his carry-on on it instead.

He went to the bathroom and splashed cold water on his face.

He snatched a hand towel from the rack and wiped his face dry.

He heard a noise.

He went back out and realized the sound was coming from his carry-on.

He checked his bag and found that the cell phone Travers had given him was ringing.

"Solaire," he said, answering.

"I'm glad you made it safely to New York. I hope Customs and Immigration didn't give you a problem."

"Thanks to you, they didn't."

"And where are you staying, if I may ask?"

"A hotel."

"It would be nice to know which one, considering we are paying for it."

"The Ritz-Carlton."

"Pricey."

"Like you said, you're paying for it."

"The grand opening of Crystal Towers is tomorrow night. If I were you, I would be there."

"Okay."

"And Mr. Solaire…"

"Yes?"

"I would be very careful."

The line went dead.

***

Solaire left the hotel and headed for the first place on his agenda: Brooks Brothers on Madison Avenue.

A short, slim, and exceptionally dressed man assisted Solaire in choosing a suit. From their 1818 Collection, Solaire picked a Fitzgerald two-button, dark gray suit, with a Bengal stripe dress shirt and a navy blue and gold striped tie. He chose exquisitely polished black leather dress shoes to go with the suit.

Solaire left his purchases so the man could tailor the suit to his body size, and he headed to the next location on his agenda: a printing shop.

He ordered a dozen business cards and left.

Along the way, Solaire stopped at a business that provided a telephone answering service.

He grabbed a chicken falafel from a food truck and headed for his last destination.

He chewed the bread and meat and stared across the street at a building.

The place was magnificent. A steel structure with a glass exterior that rose high up into the sky, and when looked at from afar, it resembled a fine piece of jewelry. Workers came and went, scrambling to get the place ready for the grand opening.

Solaire finished the last bite of his falafel and threw away the wrapper. Then he headed for Crystal Towers.

He spotted a man who looked like he was in charge. He was wearing an open-collared suit and was barking orders.

"When is the party?" Solaire asked, going up to him.

"Tomorrow night," the man answered.

"How does one get into it?"

"By invitation only."

The man became distracted and began arguing with another man. Solaire took the opportunity and snuck in.

By the looks of it, there was still a lot of work to be done. Construction workers were busy sanding, painting, and installing. Interior designers were removing objects from boxes in order to set up the place. The main lobby was loud, noisy, and chaotic.

A woman in a tight dress approached Solaire. "Are you from Creative Designs with the displays?"

"No."

She shook her head and walked away.

Solaire's foot touched something. He knelt and picked it up.

It was a pamphlet for an open house for Crystal Towers. The cover had *Manhattan Realtors Inc.* on it, along with the address.

Solaire decided to pay them a visit.

Before heading there, he made one last visit to a clothing store, where he purchased white casual pants with matching loafers, a designer shirt, and a navy blue jacket to go with it. He also picked up a silver Esquire watch.

***

He walked through a door, up a flight of stairs, and found the office of Manhattan Realtors Inc.

A receptionist asked if he had an appointment.

"I don't have one," he replied. "And quite frankly, I didn't think I'd need one." Solaire injected a tinge of annoyance into his last sentence.

The receptionist politely asked him to take a seat.

He did.

The office hummed with noise. Solaire sensed that there was a lot happening in the back. Telephones were ringing, fax machines were devouring documents, and photocopiers were spitting out papers.

A woman approached him.

She introduced herself as Sandy Williams.

Her dark brown hair matched her hazel eyes, and her lips were painted red. She was wearing a black business suit.

"What can I do for you?" she asked.

Solaire held up the pamphlet he'd picked up from Crystal Towers.

Sandy smiled. "That's one of our biggest projects. Follow me."

She led him to a corner cubicle.

"You don't have an office?" Solaire asked once he was seated.

"I'm a junior agent right now," Sandy replied.

"Then maybe I should be talking to someone else."

"I can answer all of your questions." She then leaned in. "I could use the experience, you know. But all purchases and sales will be through our senior agents."

"All right," Solaire said, gently crossing his leg over the other. "Tell me a little about Crystal Towers."

"Well, as you may or may not have heard, the grand opening is tomorrow. It's located near downtown Manhattan. It was built with local labor, so all the money has gone back into the community." She seemed pleased about the last part. "It has twenty floors with a hundred units. It has your basic amenities: security, gym on each floor, entertainment rooms, a swimming pool, and a great view of the city."

"And the cost of all these amenities?" Solaire asked.

"The price ranges from one-point-five million for our smaller units to over ten million for the larger ones," Sandy replied. "But every unit is custom-made. All the fixtures are from local designers, and the best material is used on the hardwood floors, as well as the kitchen and bathroom. It also comes with everything you need as soon as you buy: fridge, stove, television, and furniture."

"Furniture?" Solaire asked, raising an eyebrow.

"It's basic but matches the designs of each unit. Naturally, if the new owners want to change it, they most certainly can."

"I should hope so," he said, "for the price they are paying."

"Are you looking for one for yourself?"

"No."

He removed his business card and placed it before her.

The card was white, and it read in gold lettering, *Roman Solaire, Procurement, Travers Property Management*. There was a Bay Area address.

Solaire said, "We at Travers Management acquire properties for our clients. Our clients are quite wealthy and are always looking at investment opportunities. We try to find investments that meet their business and financial objectives."

"How many units are you looking for?" Sandy said, feeling the gold lettering with her fingers.

"If the price is right, then as many as necessary."

"Um, I'll be right back," she said and then left.

Solaire adjusted his shirt and crossed one leg over the other.

*****

Sandy knocked on the glass door. The man behind the desk waved her in.

"What is it, Sandy? I'm busy," Patrick Carr said.

"I have a gentleman outside who is interested in purchasing units in Crystal Towers."

"Did you say *units*?"

"Yes, more than one," Sandy said.

She handed him the business card.

He examined it and then twisted to get a better view of the man sitting in one of the cubicles.

He picked up the phone and dialed the number on the card.

After one ring, a female voice answered. "Travers Property Management. How can I help you?"

After a pause, Patrick said, "Can I speak to Mr. Roman Solaire?" He read the name on the card.

"Mr. Solaire is away on business. May I know what this is about?"

"That's fine, thank you." He hung up. He turned to Sandy. "Good that you brought this to me."

He pulled on his coat, adjusted his tie, and after quickly fixing his hair, he left his office.

*****

Solaire had to stop himself from smiling once he saw the man approach.

After introducing himself, Patrick said, "Mr. Solaire, if you please, why don't we make you more comfortable in my office?"

Solaire looked around the small cubicle. "I'm quite comfortable here."

Patrick glanced over at Sandy, who was smiling.

"As a senior agent, I can better assist you."

"Ms. Williams has been doing a good job so far," Solaire said. "She seems to know what she's talking about."

"I see," Patrick said. "Then, I guess I'll leave you in her… capable hands."

Solaire said, "There is something that you might be able to do."

"Yes?" Patrick asked, sounding eager.

"I hear there is a big party tomorrow night. Maybe you can assist me in… how can I say it? Getting an invitation."

"I most certainly can do that."

Patrick left.

"Thank you," Sandy said, turning to Solaire.

"For what?"

"For giving me this opportunity."

"I haven't bought anything yet," he said.

"It doesn't matter. I just wanted to see that look on his face."

Solaire smiled.

***

The next day, Solaire was back at Manhattan Realtors Inc.

"You're back, Mr. Solaire," Sandy Williams said.

"I came for the invitation."

"I have it right here." She handed him a blue envelope.

Solaire took the envelope, snuck a quick look inside, and placed it in his inside jacket pocket.

"Have you decided if you want to look at a unit at Crystal Towers?" Sandy asked.

"About that," Solaire said. "Why don't you tell me more over lunch?"

"Are you asking me out on a date, Mr. Solaire?"

"I wouldn't dare." Solaire shook his head. "But call me Roman."

***

They found a Japanese restaurant not far from the real estate agency. They were seated on the second floor.

Like the first floor, the second floor had its own sushi bar with a chef working behind it. The restaurant walls were spring green, the wood décor was light, and the lighting was bright.

They ordered appetizers—broiled cod marinated in sake paste and crisp lily root croquettes.

Solaire picked up his chopsticks and placed a piece of cod in his mouth. "Tell me, Ms. Williams…"

"Call me, Sandy," she said, sitting across from him.

"Sandy, how long have you worked at your agency?"

"Nine months."

"Does it pay well?"

"Not as much as I hoped for, but it's a start."

"You're from here?"

"You mean Manhattan?"

He nodded while chewing.

"No." She shook her head. "I'm actually from Illinois."

"So, what is a girl from Illinois doing in a big city like New York?"

"Work. Money. Fame. Like everyone, I came for the big lights."

Solaire paused. "You mean Broadway?"

Sandy blushed. "I know it sounds so Hollywood. But yeah, I wanted to be on stage."

"Then what are you doing selling real estate?"

"I'm not actually doing any selling right now, but a girl's gotta pay the bills."

Trays containing their meals were placed in front of them. They held nine varieties of sushi, including bluefin tuna, Spanish mackerel, and shrimp and tamago.

Sandy said, "What do you do, Roman? Apart from property hunting for wealthy clients."

"I do everything." He leaned closer. "Do you want to know what I really do?"

She squinted. "Yes."

"I procure information for my clients that they otherwise might not be able to gather."

Sandy looked confused.

"For instance, I'm here in New York to get information that might give my clients the upper hand."

"You mean, whether to invest in Crystal Towers or not?"

"Precisely."

She smiled. "And here I thought you invited me for pleasure."

He smiled back. "Who said business and pleasure can't go hand in hand?"

***

"Okay," she said. "Now that I know your true motive, ask me what you like."

"Tell me about the developer of Crystal Towers."

"You mean Guy Fox?" Sandy laughed and shook her head. "He's a real piece of work."

"I'm listening."

"I shouldn't be telling you this. You're the buyer."

"I may be the buyer, but *you're* not selling me anything, are you, Sandy?"

"Yeah, I guess. Patrick does the selling," she conceded. "Okay, about Guy Fox. Wherever he goes, he doesn't go without his bodyguards."

"Why does a developer need security?"

"That's what I thought, too." She leaned in. "I think he's in business with the wrong people."

"What kind of people?"

"I don't know, but people he might need protection from."

"Why is your agency in business with him?"

"Why wouldn't they be? If they sell all the condominium units, they make millions just on commission."

"Tell me more about Fox."

"He's loud and obnoxious. I've heard him screaming at our agents. He believes we're not pushing hard enough to sell all the units. Over seventy-five percent of them have been sold already, and with the grand opening tonight, we hope to sell the remaining in the next month."

"I still have an opportunity to buy units?"

"You do, except for one."

27

Solaire waited.

"The most exclusive unit, which is located on the very top floor, Fox will keep for himself. It's really to keep his wife happy."

"He's married?"

"What I heard is that Guy Fox never does any business under his name. Everything is done through his wife."

"Why would he do that?"

"I don't know. Maybe he doesn't want his wife involved in his *other* business dealings."

"So, he cares about her?"

"Maybe just enough not to get her in trouble."

"Or to legitimize what he is doing as a developer."

She glanced at her watch. "I better get back to the office. We've got a lot of work to do for tonight." She got up. "I guess I'll see you then."

"Now that I've got my invitation, you most certainly will."

He watched her leave and waited for the bill.

Solaire thought hard about the evening to come.

At the grand opening, he might have to introduce himself to Guy Fox.

***

The man brushed Solaire's lapel and adjusted his collar. He then moved back to allow Solaire to view himself fully.

The suit fit him perfectly. The sleeves were just the right length, and the hem was cut precisely to his height.

"How do you feel, sir?" the tailor at Brooks Brothers asked.

"Like a successful property manager."

Solaire headed to his final stop.

Several salesmen got up when he entered, noticing his expensive suit.

The manager himself came out of his office and introduced himself.

"Welcome to BMW, sir," he said, extending his hand. Solaire shook it.

"Any models you have a preference for?"

"I'm not picky."

"Are you looking to buy or lease?" the manager asked.

"I'm looking to rent."

The manager looked confused. "We don't rent vehicles at this location."

"That's too bad," Solaire said. "I need it just for tonight."

"One night?"

"Yes, for the grand opening of Crystal Towers. It's a shame you don't rent, though."

The manager suddenly smiled. "We can always make exceptions. Please follow me."

He took Solaire to the back of the showroom.

"This is one of our finest models."

The black BMW 6 Series glistened under the showroom lights. It was a two-door convertible model.

"I think you would look very nice if you drove up in this," the manager said.

Solaire examined the vehicle's body. "I think I would, too."

***

The drive to Crystal Towers was quick, but the drive up to the front door was not. Cars were lined up, bumper to bumper, as they slowly made their way to the entrance.

An attendant held the BMW's door open for Solaire as he got out.

"Nice car," the attendant said.

"I know."

Crystal Towers was even more beautiful at night, glowing under the moonlight as if the light was reflecting off of a diamond.

Solaire strolled over to the red carpet and up to the two-door entrance.

He held the invitation up for a guard to see and then entered.

Loud music blared all around. A DJ was spinning records in the back.

The front lobby of the building had been transformed into a nightclub. The lights were low, and people were milling about with glasses in their hands.

Solaire spotted the makeshift bar and approached the bartender.

"Iced tea, no ice," he said.

The bartender looked at him as if he had not heard him.

Solaire said more slowly, "I'll have a glass of iced tea, but no ice in it."

When the bartender had finally comprehended Solaire's order, he moved away.

Solaire surveyed the party.

There was no sign of Guy Fox.

He felt someone beside him.

He turned.

It was Sandy Williams, and she looked exquisite. She wore a strapless black dress and high heels. Her hair was smooth and fell down her back.

"Glad you made it," she said, holding a glass.

"I wouldn't miss it for the world."

His drink came.

"Quite a party," Solaire said.

"It's *the* party to be at."

"I guess I have you to thank for it." He raised his glass.

"Not me, but him," Sandy said.

Patrick Carr approached them. "Mr. Solaire, thank you for coming."

"Thank you for inviting me." He raised his glass. Patrick raised his in return.

"Do you like what you see so far?" Patrick asked. "Manhattan Realtors can help you get the best properties at the best price."

"I don't doubt that," Solaire said. "But I don't invest my clients' money until I have at least met the developer."

Patrick understood. "Mr. Fox will be arriving soon, and I will personally introduce you to him."

"I'd appreciate that."

Patrick walked away.

"I can't stand him," Sandy said.

"He seems nice," Solaire said.

"He's nice only to his clients, not his employees."

Solaire sipped his drink and then set it down. "Do you know which way the men's room is? I would like to freshen up."

"I thought only women did that," Sandy said.

"It's the twenty-first century. The rules have changed."

She pointed to the end of the lobby.

He left her and headed in that direction. He slowed at the elevators. Two seconds before, he had seen two men in dark suits board one of them.

Solaire pulled out his cell phone and acted as if he was texting someone.

He saw the elevator stop on the twentieth floor.

Solaire then headed for the men's room, but instead of going into it, he turned and found the stairs.

He jogged up the stairs to the second floor. From there, he took the elevator to the twentieth floor.

He got off and spotted the same two men at the end of the hall.

Once they saw him, they quickly approached.

"You're not supposed to be here," one of them said.

"I bought one of the units, and I just wanted to see it," Solaire pleaded.

"Not on this floor, you didn't."

"This isn't the nineteenth?"

"Nope."

"Sorry, fellas." Solaire went back into the elevator.

He went down to the second floor and took the stairs back to the first.

He found Sandy where he'd left her.

"You're sweating," Sandy said.

"Am I?" He wiped his temples. "The bathroom was all the way in the back."

***

There was a bit of commotion near the building's entrance. Solaire turned and saw Guy Fox coming in. On his arm was a stunning woman—his wife.

She had radiant olive skin, jet black hair, and dazzling dark eyes.

Guy Fox, on the other hand, looked exactly like his picture. His head and face were clean-shaven, He was of slight build, and in-person, he looked much taller.

The couple smiled as they were greeted by the guests. Solaire noticed how Fox's bodyguards discretely blended with the crowd.

"They sure know how to make an entrance," Sandy said, sipping her drink.

After a few minutes of pleasantries, a microphone was handed to Fox. "Thank you, friends, and honored guests. I can't say enough what a pleasure it is—on my wallet—to finally see Crystal Towers complete." There was a smattering of laughter. "It's been a four-year journey, one I thought would never end. But after two delays, we are finally able to say we have one of the most luxurious buildings in all of New York." There were cheers. "It has always been one of my dreams to develop a project in Manhattan, and I would like to thank all those who have worked hard in making this dream of mine come true." Fox smiled at his wife. She smiled back in return. "I think this would also be a good time to especially thank the new owners who bought units at Crystal Towers." There were a few hoots and even a whistle. "Without you, this building would have never existed." More laughter. "Enjoy tonight. Tomorrow you will all receive the keys to your new homes. I hope Crystal Towers is everything you have ever wanted and more."

Guy Fox put down the microphone and began shaking hands with the other guests.

Solaire finished his drink.

Patrick brought Fox over. "Mr. Fox, I would like you to meet Mr. Roman Solaire."

They shook hands.

"Mr. Solaire is looking at investment opportunities for his wealthy clients," Patrick said.

Fox smiled. "We welcome that."

"I've heard great things about Crystal Towers from Sandy here," Solaire said.

Fox turned to Sandy, unsure who she was.

Patrick quickly interjected, "Sandy Williams works at Manhattan Realtors."

Fox just smiled.

Solaire said, "I prefer to know who I'm buying from before I do it."

"Understandable," Fox said. "I don't do any business unless I've met the other person myself."

Solaire's mind flashed back to the photo of Fox with the African man.

"Indeed," Solaire replied.

"Why don't you drop by my office tomorrow, and I'll try to alleviate any concerns that you may have," Fox said.

"I would appreciate that."

Suddenly, a woman appeared beside Fox.

"Mr. Solaire," Fox said, "let me introduce my wife, Jackie Belafonte."

The woman extended her hand.

Solaire took her hand and, with a slight bow, said, "A pleasure."

She smiled. There was something mesmerizing about her. It was as if she knew what she wanted and how to get it.

Solaire could tell that Fox was enamored with her.

"Excuse us," Fox said.

Fox and his wife moved away, resuming mingling with their guests.

***

"So," Sandy said, turning to him, "what should we do for the rest of the evening?"

Solaire said, "I would like to see New York."

Sandy looked at her watch. "I know just the thing. Come, we don't have much time."

The attendant brought the BMW to the curb, and after Solaire tipped him, they got in.

"Where to?" he asked.

"The Rockefeller Center," Sandy answered.

After purchasing their tickets, they took the last elevator to the seventieth floor.

The Top of the Rock, a deck on top of the Rockefeller building, allowed an open-air, unobstructed, 360-degree view of New York.

The view was breathtaking at night, and Solaire couldn't help feeling like he was at the top of the world.

The air was chilly. Solaire took off his coat and placed it around Sandy's shoulders.

"Thank you," she said.

"Thank you for bringing me here."

Solaire could see the Empire State Building, Central Park, the Chrysler Building, and in the distance, the Statue of Liberty.

The city looked vibrant and alive.

"When I came to New York," Sandy said, "I felt like I didn't belong here. The city felt like it was moving faster than me, and I couldn't keep up with it. I felt like I was falling behind. But then one day I came here and saw this, and I knew I wanted to be here. I made myself a promise that I would make something of myself, and I would do it here."

"I hope you do," Solaire said sincerely.

Sandy smiled. "I feel weird telling you this. I really don't know much about you."

"What would you like to know?"

"Is there a Mrs. Solaire or even a Mrs. Solaire-in-waiting somewhere?"

"In my line of work, there just wouldn't be a place for a missus."

"Your work is your life?"

"Sometimes, I feel my work will lead to the end of my life."

Solaire was glad Sandy didn't ask what he meant.

The breeze was cool as it brushed passed her hair. "The night is so beautiful," she said.

"It would be even more beautiful with a kiss," Solaire said.

She turned to him.

He smiled.

"You're dangerous, Mr. Roman Solaire," she said.

"Call me Danger Man."

She smiled.

They kissed.

***

When Solaire entered his room, he heard a noise. He knew exactly what it was.

"Yes," Solaire said, answering the cell phone.

"I'm glad you are enjoying New York," replied the voice. It was Travers.

"It's a great city," Solaire said.

"I hope you still remember why you are there in the first place."

"I do. I'm here to search for something that no one knows exists."

"You sound frustrated," Travers said.

"I am." Solaire sat on the bed. "I don't enjoy playing with other people."

"You mean that woman, Sandy Williams?" Travers asked.

Solaire's back arched. "How do you know about her? Are you watching me?"

"I'm not interested in your personal life, but I am interested in your progress. In any case, use her as an asset to complete your mission."

Solaire almost laughed. "You sound like a government man."

There was no response.

"Let me make something very clear," Solaire said. "I do not work for any government or country. I am not some secret agent who manipulates others for the greater good."

"Then what do you do, Mr. Solaire?"

Solaire was silent.

"Let me clarify," Travers said. "If you don't work for an agency, then what is it that you do?"

"I don't know," Solaire said.

"Let me tell you what you do. You are good at finding that one thing that otherwise may never be found. You have the ability to search relentlessly, through any obstacles that get in your way, to locate that which you have been hired to find. I've been watching you for some time. I was highly impressed at how you were able to reunite that woman with her daughter."

Solaire's mind flashed back. A woman had found him somehow and begged him to find her daughter, who had gone missing eighteen years earlier. The police had given up, but she had not. It took Solaire six months to track the girl, but not before rooting himself in the small town the girl was in. It was the girl's neighbor who had taken her and raised the girl as her own. The townsfolk had become so enamored with Solaire that one of them led him straight to the girl, who was now a twenty-year-old woman.

Travers said, "You had no problem manipulating the townspeople at that time."

"I knew what I was searching for, and I knew what I was doing was right. I *don't* know you. I *don't* know who you work for, and I *don't* know if what I'm doing is right."

There was silence on the other end. "I know you don't know me or my employers, so you have no reason to believe me, but I assure you that if what you were doing was wrong, then I wouldn't be part of it."

The line went dead.

Solaire frowned.

***

The next morning, Solaire was back at Crystal Towers, but this time he was dressed in a uniform.

Even after the grand opening, there was still work being done, from landscaping to renovating to home inspecting.

Solaire took the elevator all the way to the top.

He got off, and as he expected, he was confronted by two men in suits.

"Can I help you?" one said.

"Yeah, I'm from the city." Solaire quickly flashed a badge. "I'm inspecting all units in the building, and I need to inspect that one." He pointed to the suite they were guarding.

"What for?"

"To make sure that it is energy-efficient."

The guard glanced at his partner, unsure.

"Hey, listen," Solaire said. "I have to make sure that this building is in compliance with the New York City Energy Conservation Code. This is mandatory stuff. If I can't do it, then I'll write up a report saying the building doesn't meet the standards, and then your boss will be in deep trouble."

The guard scanned Solaire up and down. The uniform looked official. It was. Solaire had "borrowed" it from an actual city inspector.

"Okay," the guard said. "But make it quick."

Solaire entered the suite and was taken aback by how luxurious everything was, from the frames on the walls to the marble floor to even the furniture.

*Guy Fox knows how to live in style*, Solaire thought.

Solaire quickly scanned the interior. There was a spacious living room in front, with an open kitchen to the right and a hallway to the left. A spiraling staircase led up to another floor.

Solaire felt the guard hovering behind him.

"I can do this by myself," Solaire said.

"I've got my orders."

Solaire flipped a notepad and began walking around the living room. He scribbled something down, pretending to be busy, and then went around peeking into the nooks and crannies.

Near the windows, he pulled out an object and pressed it. Brown powder sprayed from the gadget's tip.

"What's that?" the guard asked.

"It lets me know if there are any air leaks," Solaire replied.

He heard footsteps and turned.

Jackie Belafonte descended the staircase, looking as stunning as ever. She wore a full dress, but this one was more modest than the one she wore the night before.

"What's going on?" she asked the guard.

He looked nervous. "He's… he's an inspector from the city, ma'am." He looked in Solaire's direction for help.

"As part of the New York City Energy—" Solaire said.

"No, you're not."

"I'm sorry?"

"We met last night at the party," Jackie said.

Solaire remained poker-faced. "I think you have me mistaken for someone else."

"I don't think so. I never forget a face."

The guard looked in Solaire's direction. His demeanor had instantly changed from accommodating to suspicious.

"Leave us," Jackie Belafonte told the guard.

The guard looked confused.

"Now," she demanded.

***

When the guard was gone, she turned to Solaire and said, "It's Mr. Solaire, I believe. Yes?"

He gave her a slight bow.

"Can I get you a drink?" she asked.

"Iced tea, but hold the ice."

"You're not a hard drink type of man?"

Solaire shook his head. "It upsets my stomach."

"Please have a seat."

He did.

The white leather sofa was soft and comfortable.

She returned and sat across from him.

"To what do I owe the pleasure?" she asked before she took a sip from her drink.

"Well," Solaire said, "I'm not sure how I can explain this…" He pointed to his uniform.

"Don't. My husband told me about you and your interests in Crystal Towers. Isn't it extraordinary?" She moved her hand around the suite.

He nodded. "It is."

"Unlike my husband, I like theatrics."

"I'm not sure what you mean," Solaire said, confused.

"City inspector?" She raised an eyebrow. "It would have been easier if you merely requested a tour of the building."

Solaire understood. "But the tour would show me only what I need to see. This allows me to see what doesn't need to be seen."

"You sound like a private investigator. I hope your clients are paying you well."

Solaire thought of Travers. "Believe me. Money is not a concern."

She smiled. "As you can see, it's not for us, either."

"Ms. Belafonte…"

"Call me, Jackie."

"Jackie, why the guards?"

She put the glass down. "As you are aware, my husband is a very wealthy man. And in today's economic state, he is one of the few people who have actually made money in the real estate market. It's a very competitive business, and there are some who will do anything to get ahead." She sighed.

"You sound like you don't want to be part of it?"

"Don't get me wrong. Who doesn't like luxury? But I have interests other than my husband."

Solaire waited.

"Charity," Jackie said. "The Jackie B. Foundation donates food and clothing to children all over Africa. My husband's passion is real estate, while mine is helping those in need."

"I'm sure your husband's work helps you with yours."

Jackie was silent for a moment. "It does," she finally said.

Solaire got up. "Thank you for your time and your hospitality."

***

Solaire was having lunch at a diner when he noticed a man across the street. The man was wearing a large trench coat, black sunglasses propped up on his nose, and an old-style press hat on his head.

The man stuck out like a sore thumb amongst the urban and hip crowd. He looked like a spy from a Cold War novel.

The man kept looking in Solaire's direction.

Solaire finished his beef sandwich, gulped down the iced tea, and went to the back of the diner.

Instead of going into one of the bathrooms, he turned left and went straight through the kitchen. He apologized to the staff, who were shocked to see him, and exited through the back.

He circled around the building.

The man was no longer standing where Solaire had last seen him. Instead, he was standing in front of the diner, peering through the window.

Solaire approached him from behind and stuck two fingers into his back.

"Don't turn around," Solaire said in a deep voice.

The man was startled.

"Follow me," Solaire commanded.

He obliged.

They walked down the street and into an alley.

"Turn," Solaire instructed.

The man did so.

He was middle-aged, slightly overweight, and he had green eyes, which now looked concerned.

"Who are you?" Solaire demanded.

"Are you going to shoot me?" the man asked.

"It'll depend on your answers. Why are you following me?"

"I was asked to."

"By whom?"

"I can't say."

"You better start talking or else—"

"Listen, I…" Suddenly the man stopped. His body relaxed, and he smiled. "You don't have a real gun."

"Are you sure?" Solaire said.

"I am."

"You want to bet your life on it?"

"No, but I'm pretty sure of it, Mr. Solaire."

Solaire removed his hand from his pocket.

"How do you know my name?" he asked.

"Mr. Travers told me."

Solaire almost laughed. "He sent you to watch me?"

"No." He shook his head. "To assist you."

"I don't need help."

"That's not for me to decide."

"You go back and tell Travers that I work alone."

"I have my orders."

"I *don't*," Solaire said. "I can handle this myself."

The man shrugged. "That's fine by me. I get paid either way. Plus, New York is a nice place to visit. Can you recommend any fun attractions while I'm here?"

Solaire paused.

"Donald Levack," the man said, extending his hand.

Solaire didn't take it.

"Listen, I get it," Levack said. "You're a lone wolf. You like to hunt by yourself."

Solaire wasn't sure where this was going.

"Like you, I'm a lone beast too. How about this? I do my thing, and you do yours."

"What is it that you do?" Solaire finally asked.

"Let's just say, if I were the one bringing you into this alley, talking is something we wouldn't be doing."

Solaire understood. "You're a hitman."

Levack cringed. "I don't like that word. It's so sinister. I prefer to think that I get things done."

"Whatever you are, you don't hide very well." Solaire moved his eyes up and down Levack's attire.

"Really?" Levack looked surprised. "I thought it made me mysterious."

"Maybe in a book, but not in real life."

Solaire started to move away.

"You wanna go for a drink?" Levack asked.

"No, thanks. You stay away from me." Solaire stopped at the end of the alley. "And tell Travers not to send anyone else to help me."

***

Solaire stormed down the street with his hands in his pockets and his head down. He moved past pedestrians who were busy enjoying the many sights and sounds of New York City. Vendors lined the streets, hawking everything from designer sunglasses to personalized T-shirts to stylized artwork.

Solaire stopped at one vendor's booth. Movie posters lined the wall.

"Them are all originals, brother," said the seller.

The posters ranged from the classics to the contemporary.

"I give you the best price in the city," the seller said.

Solaire glanced to the left and stopped.

A red-haired man wearing black clothes and a black jacket stood nearby, staring in his direction.

*Not another one of Travers' goons*, Solaire thought.

But there was something different about the man. He made no effort to hide himself from Solaire.

"What you like, brother?" the seller asked, interrupting his thoughts. "James Bond? Indiana Jones? *Die Hard*?"

"No, thanks."

Solaire turned and began walking in the other direction.

He sensed the man was following behind.

Whoever he was, Solaire didn't want to find out.

Solaire quickly crossed the street and hurried his steps.

He noticed the man did not cross but kept pace on the other side.

Solaire turned sharply around the corner. He then dashed down the block, narrowly missing pedestrians.

When he had passed two full blocks, he stopped and glanced back.

The man was nowhere to be found.

Solaire controlled his breathing.

He quickly steadied his heartbeat.

*This was too easy*, he thought.

His instincts were correct.

A block away, the man reappeared.

They both locked eyes.

The man went into a full sprint. Solaire did the same in the opposite direction.

Up ahead at the end of the block were stairs leading down to the subway.

Solaire sped up, aiming for the steps.

Suddenly a black SUV appeared around the corner, cutting him off.

Solaire tried to maneuver around the vehicle, but someone pushed him from behind.

The momentum propelled him forward, straight to the SUV's open doors.

A man grabbed him. Another placed a bag over his head.

He was shoved into the back seat.

His hands were fastened together.

Solaire felt the SUV lurch forward and then squeal away.

***

The bag was pulled off his head. A chill hit his damp face.

He blinked.

It was dark.

A bright light was flashed in his eyes, blinding him.

He squinted.

Two more lights were turned on.

He quickly took his situation in.

He was seated on a chair with his wrists tied behind his back.

He moved his head around.

He was in a room, but where?

Then it dawned on him. The metallic sounds emanating from the walls informed him that he was in a shipping container.

Solaire shivered.

It wasn't particularly cold, but the feeling of emptiness made him so.

Behind the strobe lights, a figure emerged from the shadows.

It took Solaire a second to recognize him.

It was Guy Fox.

"You have not been honest with me, Mr. Solaire," Fox said, standing before him. "If that is your real name."

"It's the name I go by," Solaire said.

Fox's lips curled into a smile. "I'm sure."

"Is this how you conduct your business?" Solaire asked.

"No, but you're not really a businessman, are you?" Fox smiled again.

"I don't know what you mean."

"I'm sure you don't." Fox walked around him, his hands behind his back as if he were a teacher reprimanding a student who had been a very naughty boy.

A chair was placed in front of Solaire. Fox sat down.

Behind him, Solaire glimpsed the red-haired man.

There was a twinkle in the man's eyes.

Fox crossed one leg over the other and said, "My wife told me you had dropped by *unexpectedly*."

"It was for my business."

"Ah, yes," Fox said. He pulled out a card from his jacket pocket. "Travers Property Management. How fascinating. What is it that you do? Let me remember. You provide investment opportunities to your clients, yes? Well, we called the number, and we spoke to a very nice woman. She assured us that Travers Property Management did, in fact, exist, but she failed to realize who she was talking to." Fox's smile widened. "I know people who know other people. We sent someone to the address and, surprise, surprise, there is no Travers Property Management. Why is that, now?"

"I can assure you there is a Mr. Travers," Solaire interjected.

"And who is he?"

"I wish I knew."

Fox adjusted his jacket. "Then let me ask… who are *you*?"

"You already know my name."

"Okay, then what do you want from me?"

"Information."

"Information?"

"Yes. You are funding terrorism in Africa, and I want to know how."

"Terrorism?" Fox almost looked offended.

"We have photos of you with known terrorists in Angola, Sudan, Congo; the list goes on."

Fox paused and sized Solaire up. "Yes, it's true that I've been in those countries, but not for the reasons you think."

"Then for what?"

"Business relations."

"You can call it whatever you like."

Fox's eyes narrowed. "It is unwise to accuse someone when you are in the position you are in now."

Solaire fidgeted, but the restraints held tight.

Fox said, "Even if you found something that somehow linked me to the crimes that you are accusing me of, what could you do? I am an American citizen. I cannot be extradited. Who has the authority to prosecute me, except for the Department of Justice? And—" Fox leaned forward, "—they won't do anything about crimes outside US soil."

Solaire didn't have an answer.

"Plus, I'm a citizen in good standing." Fox beamed proudly. "If you had stayed at the grand opening, I would have introduced you to the mayor."

The restraints cut into Solaire's wrists.

"Who do you work for?" Fox asked.

"I don't work for anyone."

Fox almost laughed. "You take me for a fool, Mr. Solaire? You want me to believe that you are here, on your own, to find some evidence that links me to crimes in another continent?"

Solaire said nothing.

"I was wrong about you. I thought you were a smart man, but we all make errors in our judgment." Fox got up. "The biggest error you made is believing that I'm involved in terrorism." Fox got closer, their faces inches apart. "Look at my eyes. Do I look like someone who is capable of that?"

"We are all capable of much worse," Solaire said.

Fox nodded and moved away. "You are right, I suppose. For what it's worth, I am only a businessman—nothing more, nothing less. My ambitions have nothing to do with what happens in another country or continent, for that matter. I'm only interested in making money and leaving my mark in this world. My buildings will outlive me. And if you want to outlive anyone else, Mr. Solaire, my advice would be for you to take up another line of work."

Fox moved to the edge of the light. "One more thing. There was another person I caught trying to meddle in my affairs. He was found shot many times. I assure you that I had nothing to do with it. It is, however, regrettable what happened to him. But I suspect he had other enemies than me, and they weren't very forgiving." Fox turned to the red-haired man. "Show Mr. Solaire our hospitality and then send him on his way."

Fox disappeared into the shadows.

***

When the metallic door of the shipping container closed, the red-haired man turned to Solaire.

He had a smile on his face. It was both menacing and threatening.

He rubbed his knuckles and tightened his fist.

He swung hard at Solaire's face.

The impact knocked Solaire and the chair over.

Blood spurted out of his upper lip.

The man lifted him up and placed him back in a sitting position.

Solaire could taste the blood in his mouth.

He spat it out.

"Okay, I get the point," Solaire said. "Are we done?"

The red-haired man smiled, this time revealing his crooked teeth. "No, Mr. Solaire, we are just getting started."

He swung the back of his fist across Solaire's temple.

The pain shot through Solaire's head.

Solaire tried to shake it off.

The side of his face burned, and his temple ached and throbbed.

The next hit was straight to the midsection.

Solaire almost keeled over.

He coughed.

Blood shot up his throat. He vomited.

"You are making such a mess," the man said.

Between breaths, Solaire said, "Then maybe you should stop."

"Maybe you should just die first."

"Your boss wouldn't like that."

"He's too soft," the man said. "Our orders don't come from him."

He swung again, and again.

Then he pulled out his gun and aimed it at Solaire, who was barely able to keep his eyes open.

"Two bullets," the man said. "That's all I need for you. The last guy was a professional. He required many, many more."

Solaire made no attempt at a response. The look on the man's face told him what was next.

"The last guy thought he was some sort of spy." The man snickered. "He worked in secrecy, like he was in a covert operation, so no one asked too many questions when they found his body looking like Swiss cheese. But you are different. You made yourself known to everyone." The man lowered the gun. "Making you disappear will be much harder." He then leaned closer. "If I were you, I would go back to wherever I came from."

With the butt of the gun, the red-haired man hit Solaire across the head, blacking him out.

*****

He felt something wet on his cheek. First, it was droplets, and then it came on heavy.

Within seconds his face was soaked.

He opened his eyes and blinked.

It was raining and hard.

He was on his side, lying on a hard surface. He felt it and found it was wooden.

He heard noises in the distance.

He pushed himself up.

He was on a bench, surrounded by trees.

A man and a woman were walking toward him, laughing as they sought to escape the rain.

When they got near, the man looked at Solaire. His eyes widened with shock. The woman gasped.

"You okay, buddy?" the man asked.

"Where am I?" Solaire asked.

"Central Park."

Solaire's entire body hurt. His face probably looked much worse.

The man eyed him. "You sure you're okay?"

"I'm fine. Thank you."

"I can call 9-1-1."

"I just need to get home."

***

The cab driver dropped him off at the Ritz-Carlton's entrance. The doorman was shocked to see him enter, but Solaire brushed by him before he could say anything.

He caught the elevator up.

An old woman wearing an expensive mink coat and fine jewelry stared at him. Even her little dog kept his big round eyes trained suspiciously on him.

He got off on the fourteenth floor and went to his room.

He slowly and painfully removed his clothes.

He then went into the bathroom to survey the damage.

It wasn't as bad as he had imagined. It was worse.

Solaire's face was covered in cuts and bruises.

He cleaned his wounds with a hand towel. Pain shot through him whenever he took a deep breath.

Dark purplish patches were at the top and sides of his stomach.

His ribs weren't broken—that would have been too painful to bear—but they were bruised. So was his midsection.

He avoided touching them.

He turned on the shower and let cold water flow over his battered body.

He pulled on a bathrobe and went out.

He sat on the edge of the bed.

His mind was too exhausted to think.

He placed his head on the soft pillow.

He closed his eyes.

Within seconds, Solaire was fast asleep.

***

A noise woke him up.

It was annoying but familiar.

Solaire tried ignoring it, but it was relentless.

He pushed himself off the bed and went to the writing desk.

He picked the phone up and said, "What do you want, Travers?"

"I'm glad you are still alive, Mr. Solaire."

"I'm glad, too."

"I hope the damage wasn't permanent," Travers said.

"I'll have to wait and find out."

"It seems this may have been too much for you to handle."

"I can handle it just fine."

"Even after all that you have endured?" Travers sounded surprised.

"Yes."

"I did send help."

"You mean an assassin."

"He can be whatever you like him to be."

Solaire felt rage boil up inside him. "If you wanted Fox dead, then why send me?"

"No, we do *not* want Fox dead. Please get that straight. If we wanted him dead, he would have been dead years ago. We want him alive."

"Then why send Donald Levack?"

"He's not there to kill Guy Fox. He's there so that *you* don't get killed."

"It sounds like you care, Travers."

"I don't. We just don't need another dead body."

"You mean the previous man you sent?"

"He was an agent with another organization—British intelligence. They had sent us their best man, but what happened to him was unfortunate."

"The same could have happened to me. And where was Levack when I was getting my face pummeled?"

"You're still alive, aren't you?"

Solaire didn't know what to say.

Travers said, "I'm afraid I may have overestimated your abilities. It was, perhaps, not right to put you in this situation."

"I can finish it."

"I'm sure you think you can, but it has gotten very dangerous. We don't need another casualty on our hands."

"I can, and I will finish this."

"Are you sure?"

"Something doesn't add up, and I need to find out what that is."

***

Solaire went back to bed and closed his eyes.

His mind was racing now, analyzing everything that had transpired earlier.

Body language, specific conversations, what was said, and most importantly, what was not. All was now very crucial.

He had missed something.

But what was it?

He had been very careful in planning out his investigation.

Soon his mind grew foggy, and he fell asleep.

There was a knock.

His eyes snapped open.

He listened.

Someone was at the door.

He painfully jumped to his feet.

The knock came again.

He went into the bathroom and removed the metal rod from the towel hanger.

He approached the door.

"Who is it?"

"There's a package for you, sir," a male voice said.

*At this late hour*? Solaire thought.

"Sorry to bother you, but it was dropped off just now, and it says it's urgent."

Solaire opened the door.

A boyish-looking man wearing a white jacket stood smiling. He was holding a brown box.

"Thank you," Solaire said, taking it. "Remind me to tip you next time."

Solaire shut the door, and after locking it, he went to the writing desk.

He examined the box.

It was the size of a hardcover book.

Solaire weighed it on his palm. It was slightly heavy.

He gently tore the side, pulled open the flap, and extracted a piece of paper.

It was a handwritten note that read, *This might be useful next time.*

Solaire placed his fingers inside the box and pulled out a gun.

It was silver and compact, but with a good grip.

Solaire immediately knew who it was from.

Travers.

He placed the gun back inside the box, sealed it, and called the concierge desk.

When the same boyish-looking man appeared, Solaire tipped him and said, "Send it back. It's for someone else."

Solaire went to bed.

***

Solaire sat on the patio of a restaurant, sipping his iced tea.

It was mid-morning, the sun was bright, and the streets were packed with people rushing by. The roads were even worse. The traffic congestion was making motorists chomp at each other's throats. There were honks, curses, and the occasional waving of the middle finger.

Solaire observed it all through his dark sunglasses.

He sensed a man sit down at his table.

"I didn't think you'd show up," Solaire said.

"I didn't think you'd still be in New York," Donald Levack said.

A waitress showed up.

"I'll have what he's having," Levack told her.

"I thought you were a drinking man," Solaire said.

"I used to be, but I've been sober for eight years now."

"Congratulations."

"Best thing I ever did." Levack's drink came. He took a sip. "How come there's no ice in it?" he asked the waitress.

"You asked for what he had," she replied.

"Bring me some ice. The more, the better."

The waitress took the drink back.

Levack turned to Solaire. "What kind of man doesn't put ice in his drink?"

"This kind." Solaire smiled and sipped his iced tea.

Once his beverage was returned, Levack said, "You had a hell of a night."

"You could say that. I spoke to Travers, and from what I gather, you were supposed to watch me."

"Who said I wasn't?"

Solaire looked at him.

"Check your pocket."

Solaire placed his hand in his jacket and pulled out a small device.

"I snuck it into your pocket when we were in the alley."

"You heard everything?"

"Loud and clear. I gotta say, though, you took one heck of a beating."

"And you didn't think to interfere?"

"Nah, I knew you could handle it." Levack squinted and examined him up and down. "Yep, you look like you're still in one piece."

"What if I was in actual danger?"

"Oh, then I would have rode in on my horse and rescued you."

"I'm glad to hear that."

Solaire finished his drink.

Levack said, "I hear you're not a member of any agency. Is that right?"

"Yep."

"Not even CSIS?"

Solaire laughed. "The Canadian Security Intelligence Service wouldn't know what to do with me."

"*I* don't know what to do with you," Levack said.

Solaire looked at him.

Levack looked at Solaire. "Listen, I was told to fly here and help you find something."

"Travers told you?"

"Yeah, who else?"

"What are you, CIA?"

"Used to be. There's not much use for forty-year-old agents anymore."

Solaire looked at him again.

Levack rolled his eyes. "Forty-*ish*, all right?"

"You have family?" Solaire asked.

"Whoa, let's not get too chummy. We're not friends. No personal questions. Agreed?"

"All right." Solaire got up. "I have to go."

"What do you want me to do?" Levack asked.

"Right now, nothing," Solaire replied.

***

Solaire waited for her outside Manhattan Realtors.

She came out smiling, but it quickly faded once she saw him. "What happened to your face?" Sandy asked.

"Can we talk?"

"Do you want to come in?" she asked.

"It'd be better if I don't."

They walked down the street.

"I need your help," he said.

"Okay," she said, unsure.

"But first, I have to be honest with you." Solaire faced her. "I'm not into real estate."

"I kind of knew that," Sandy said with a shrug.

"You did?"

"For a big-time investor, you were too nice. Most of these guys only care about dollars and cents—more dollars than cents, though. They'd never spend time with a junior agent because they know it's the senior agents who get the big deals made."

Solaire couldn't help but smile.

"So, what are you?" she asked.

"I'm someone who is trying to find information on Guy Fox."

"Okay. What type of information?"

"I need the list of names of individuals and businesses that invested in Crystal Towers."

Sandy made a face. "That's going to be tough."

"I know, and I wouldn't have asked if there was any other way."

"Why Fox?"

"We feel he is in association with the wrong people."

"*We?*"

"I thought I was working alone, but I'm not anymore."

"And who do you work for?"

"I've been asked that before, and I wish I knew. After this is over, I'm going to have a lot of questions of my own."

They stopped at the end of the block.

"Is it Fox that did that to you?" she asked.

"It was, but I don't think he wanted it to go this far." Solaire touched his upper lip.

Sandy stared at him. "Who are you, Mr. Roman Solaire?"

He didn't know how to respond.

"You show up unexpectedly. You make a girl feel like a diamond. And then you ask her to do something that could get her in deep trouble."

"Didn't I say, 'Call me Danger Man?'"

"You are dangerous." She eyed him. "But I'll help you."

"That's good to hear, but may I ask why?"

"I always had a feeling Fox was involved in something, and it'd be nice to know what that is."

"When can you have the list?" he asked.

"It'll involve going through Patrick, but I'll try to get it to you as soon as possible."

"The sooner, the better. I'm not supposed to be in New York anymore."

***

Solaire was back at Manhattan Realtors, but this time he met Sandy a block away.

She handed him a maroon folder.

"All the investors' names are in there," she said.

"Thank you," he said.

"Thank me afterward," she said.

Without looking in it, he stuffed the folder in his jacket.

Sandy returned to her job. Solaire found a quiet spot inside a café.

After ordering a coffee, he pored over the list.

Twenty minutes later, he closed the folder.

The list was useless. It contained names of numbered companies, meaning the payments could be from anyone, be they African terrorists or yuppie investors, and tracking them would not be easy.

It never was, Solaire knew.

Solaire left the café and used a pay phone to call Levack.

He found him standing outside an electronics shop window staring at a 52-inch LCD TV.

"That one would look perfect in my living room," Levack said.

"And where would I find this living room of yours?" Solaire asked.

Levack smiled. "Now wouldn't you like to know that."

Solaire quickly got down to business. "I have the list that contains the names of companies that invested in Crystal Towers, but it's useless."

"Okay," Levack said, hoping for more.

"It does give us the name under which Crystal Towers is being developed: the Jackie B. Group."

"Isn't that the name of his wife?" Levack asked.

"Yes."

"He must really trust her."

"Or he's very careful." Solaire looked at Levack. "Apart from being a professional hitman, can you do other things?"

Levack frowned. "First… I don't like the way you phrased that, and two… yes, I can be accommodating in other ways."

"Can you get me the bank accounts of the Jackie B. Group?"

Levack thought for a moment. "I can make some calls."

"And I need it urgently."

"I'm beginning to think you always do."

***

The office was located in the back of a commercial building.

Solaire had to go up three flights of stairs and down a narrow hall to reach the place.

Rizzuto & Sons Construction was not busy save for an old lady answering a telephone.

Solaire approached her.

She was speaking fast and in another language. It took Solaire a minute to realize it was Italian.

When she hung up, he said, "Hello, I'm looking for the owner."

"Why?" the woman asked in a heavy Italian accent.

Solaire removed the Travers Property Management card from his wallet and showed it to her.

"You want to do business?" she asked.

He nodded.

She got up and went around to the back.

A few minutes later, she returned, followed by a man.

He had thick white hair, a protruding belly, and big, rough hands.

"I'm Mario," he said. He, too, had a heavy Italian accent.

"My name is Roman Solaire. Can we talk?"

Mario took him to a congested office. The room was filled with all sorts of construction materials.

"What can I do for you?" Mario asked, taking a seat.

"You worked on Crystal Towers, yes?"

Hearing the name, Mario's face turned red. "Big mistake of my life," he said.

"The day before the grand opening, I saw you arguing with a man."

"I argue with lots of people."

"He was wearing a suit and giving orders."

"Oh, that was Anthony. He hire my company."

"Where can I find him?"

"He lives in Crystal Towers."

"What do you know about Guy Fox?" Solaire quickly asked.

Mario's face turned red again. "He is sneaky, like a fox. And he is a crook." He pulled open a drawer, retrieved a file, opened it, and placed it in front of Solaire. The file contained yellow invoices. "See. This is the work I do. I put tiles in half of the bathrooms in the building."

"And you were never paid?" Solaire asked.

"I was, but they promised to pay more if I did the job by the time of the opening. I told them it was too early and I cannot do it. They said they would give me bonus if I did. I hire more people out of my pocket, and when the job finish, they don't pay me."

"You have a contract?"

"Not for the bonus." He shrugged. "I'm an honest guy. If I give you my word that I finish job, then I do it. I take Guy Fox word that he pay me. He is lying bastard."

"You didn't try to get the money?"

"I did. I send my son, Maurizio, and they beat him up."

"You didn't go to the police?"

"Everybody knows Guy Fox, even the mayor. I am just a small businessman. I am nobody." Mario looked at Solaire's face. "He owe you money too?"

Solaire touched the cut on his upper lip. "You can say that. That's why I'm here. I need your help."

Mario leaned forward, interested.

"When you were working at Crystal Towers, did they give you a master key?"

"Yes."

"Do you still have it?"

Mario's left eyebrow rose. "Yes."

"Can I have it?"

Mario leaned back in his chair. "You want the master key to Crystal Towers?"

Solaire nodded and smiled.

"Why I should give you?"

"I can get your money."

"How?"

"Leave that to me."

"Why I should trust you?"

Solaire pointed to his face.

Mario understood. He opened the drawer again and pulled out a small black box. He unlocked it with a key and then placed another key in front of Solaire.

Solaire took the key.

"You get me my money, and I say I never saw you."

***

With the key in his hand, Solaire considered whether to go back to Crystal Towers or not. More specifically, to Guy Fox's unit on the top floor. The guards would recognize him, and more importantly, this time, they wouldn't be very forgiving.

But he needed to get access to Fox's home.

Right now, he was stuck at a dead end.

If there was something, it had to be safely hidden inside that suite. But how would he get in and out?

Levack approached him.

"You have it?" Solaire asked.

"It took some arm twisting…" Levack began.

Solaire's eyes narrowed.

"No, I didn't shoot anyone, but to expedite it, I had to be a little… *demanding*." Levack held out the envelope for him.

"I don't want to know."

Solaire took the envelope and began scanning the bank statements.

"I never took you for an accountant," Levack said.

Solaire ignored him.

"I did have a look at it," Levack continued, "and there are many pages of deposits, withdrawals, transfers, payments, and so forth. Not exciting stuff. Honestly, if I had a job where I had to go through that each and every day, I would put a bullet through my head."

Solaire flipped a page, stopped, flipped back, and then flipped forward again.

"You find something?" Levack asked.

"There is money being transferred to the Jackie B. Foundation."

"So?"

"Why is the corporation using investors money to donate to a charity? A charity they control."

"I don't get it?"

"Wouldn't it be easier to collect funds straight for the foundation instead of having the money go into the corporation's account and then to the foundation?"

Levack shrugged. "Maybe it's a tax thing."

"I have a feeling it's more than that." Solaire flipped more pages. "It's a lot of money being transferred to a charity."

"Maybe Fox is a philanthropist."

"I doubt that. From our last meeting, he made it quite clear that he was a businessman, looking to make a mark on the world."

Solaire placed the statements back in the envelope.

"Now what?" Levack asked.

Solaire thought for a moment. "I have to go back to Crystal Towers."

Levack's eyes narrowed. "You sure about that? They used your face as a punching bag."

"I will not be visiting Fox's home. I have someone else in mind." Solaire turned to Levack. "You want to help?"

Levack clapped his hands. "Do I ever."

***

Donald Levack entered Crystal Towers and went straight to the security guard.

"Hi, you gotta help me," Levack said, out of breath. "I live on the eleventh floor, and I forgot my access card to parking. I've got my car running outside, and I don't need to tell you that I'm gonna get a ticket if I don't move it."

"What's your name?" the security guard asked.

"Look." Levack pointed across the street at one of the many cars parked there. "My car will get a ticket unless I get access to parking."

"Sir," the guard said, "I need your name."

"My name?" Levack sounded offended. "I bought a very expensive unit in this building, and you don't know who I am?"

"I'm sorry, sir, but I can't help you unless—"

"Fine." Levack raised his voice. "Guy will hear about this."

A concerned look swept over the guard's face. "You know Mr. Fox?"

"Know him? I practically taught him everything he knows."

"Okay, let me see what I can do."

While the guard was busy on the phone, Solaire entered the building and quickly snuck into an elevator.

"You know what?" Levack said when Solaire was out of sight. "My wife just texted me, and she has the access card. Silly me. Keep up the good work."

Before the guard could say anything, Levack was out the door and gone.

***

Solaire took the elevator up to the eighth floor. He got off, walked down the hall, and stopped in front of a door.

He gently knocked and waited.

When there was no answer, he inserted the master key and entered.

The apartment was relatively small compared to the other units in the building, but it was still luxurious with its fine carpet, leather furnishings, and expensive paintings.

Solaire sat on the leather sofa and waited.

Fortunately, he didn't have to wait long.

The door handle slowly turned.

Anthony Scottson entered.

Anthony shut the door, locked it, and proceeded further into his home.

He saw Solaire and froze.

Solaire got up, his hand still in his pocket.

"Are you armed?" Solaire asked.

Anthony shook his head. "I don't carry a gun."

"Turn around and put your hands up in the air," Solaire demanded.

Anthony did.

Solaire quickly patted him down.

He then went back and sat on the sofa.

Anthony faced him.

Solaire said, "Quietly sit down, or else they'll find your dead body in the hallway."

Anthony's face paled. He did as he was instructed.

"What… what do you want?" he asked.

"I want to know about the Jackie B. Foundation."

"It's a charity."

"Yes, I know. What do *you* do for it?"

"I administer it."

"Now, I have to ask myself, how can an administrator of a charity own a unit that costs over a million dollars?"

Anthony didn't say anything.

"I'll tell you how," Solaire continued. "He must do something that warrants substantial compensation. So, what is it that you do?"

Anthony's face tightened. "You do know *who* Jackie Belafonte is married to?"

"Yes, I think everyone knows it."

"Then, you would know that Mr. Fox would not be pleased if he found out there was someone meddling in his business."

"I think Mr. Fox is already aware."

"Then you are foolish to have come here," Anthony spat.

"Let me be the judge of that," Solaire said. "Right now, you will be foolish if you don't answer my questions."

Anthony listened.

"I know that the Jackie B. Foundation is a front for illegal activities," Solaire continued, "and I want to know what those are."

Anthony laughed. "What proof do you have of that?"

"We have your bank accounts."

"So what? What will that show?"

Solaire said nothing.

"We ship food and clothing to the needy in Africa," Anthony continued. "We are a well-respected charitable organization. And we are well-connected in New York's upper society."

Solaire said, "I just came down to inform you that we know what the foundation is being used for. We know that money is being funneled to aid terrorism. We will soon come knocking, and there will be severe consequences. My advice to you, Mr. Scottson, is to decide whose side you are on when the curtain comes down." Solaire got up. "Here is my card. If I were you, I would seriously consider speaking to us before the day comes when it is too late."

Solaire walked out.

***

As Solaire rushed down the hall, the elevator doors opened.

One of Fox's guards emerged.

Solaire doubled back and took the stairs.

He raced down, leaping over steps.

He paused and looked up. The guard was not following him.

Solaire didn't wait to see why that was.

When he was down to the third floor, the door swung open and hit him squarely in the face.

He fell back, nearly falling onto the concrete steps.

His eyes watered as pain shot up his nose.

A shadow loomed over him.

When he looked up, he saw it was the same guard.

He had a menacing look on his face.

He growled and grabbed Solaire by the neck.

He lifted Solaire up and threw him against the wall.

Solaire's back slammed into concrete, knocking the wind out of him.

The guard swung his fist at Solaire's stomach, but Solaire blocked it with his thigh.

The guard aimed for the head and swung. Solaire dropped to the ground. The fist missed and slammed into the wall.

The guard howled, clutching his hand.

Already in a crouched position, Solaire bounced and tackled him.

Solaire pushed the guard with all his might, hoping to take him over the edge and down the stairs.

He did, but the guard held on to him.

The guard slammed into the steps with Solaire on top.

They stopped when the guard's head hit the concrete at the bottom.

Solaire was disoriented.

He was still on top of the guard, who was now motionless.

Solaire shook his head. He felt dizzy.

He looked at the guard. His eyelids were open, but his eyes were rolled up. Blood oozed from the back of his head.

Solaire tried to move, but his left leg was pinned underneath the guard's body.

He pushed him off and stood up.

Pain shot down his leg.

He tried to shake it off.

He limped down the steps and onto the second floor.

When he stuck his head into the hall, he saw a guard by the elevators.

Solaire knew going through the front entrance was no longer an option.

He peeked again. The guard was pacing impatiently with his right hand on his hip.

*He's carrying a gun,* Solaire thought.

He took a deep breath and entered the hall.

He had taken two steps when the guard saw him.

The guard reached for his weapon.

Solaire quickly pulled the fire alarm.

Sirens went off.

Suddenly, a door opened.

A woman popped her head out, unsure of what was happening.

"Sorry, ma'am," Solaire said, rushing past her and into the apartment.

A man sat on a sofa watching TV.

He gaped at Solaire.

"What are you…?"

Before he could finish his sentence, Solaire grabbed a vase and threw it over the man's head.

The vase flew and shattered the sliding door in the back.

Glass flew everywhere.

Using his shoulder as protection, Solaire burst through the glass.

He took one step and then leaped off the second-floor balcony.

He landed on grass and rolled twice.

He stood up and ran as fast as he could, away from Crystal Towers.

***

"You sure that was a good idea?" Levack asked.

They were sitting in a rented Pontiac Sunfire. Crystal Towers loomed in the distance.

Solaire grabbed his ankle and grimaced. It had been taped heavily, and the painkillers hadn't kicked in yet.

"I had to spook him," Solaire replied.

"And why is that?"

"We have wasted too much time already. We need to find out how they are operating this *other* business. The best way is to apply pressure, make them do something they wouldn't normally do."

"And when they do this, you expect us to follow them?" Levack tapped the steering wheel.

Solaire nodded.

"Isn't it risky? I mean, what if we lose them?" Levack asked.

Solaire finally smiled. "That's where *your* tracking device comes in."

Levack smiled back. "I see."

"When I patted down Anthony Scottson, I snuck it into his pocket. Wherever he goes, we will know."

"I like your style." Levack rubbed his hands. "After this is over, we should go for a drink."

"I thought you didn't drink anymore?"

"I don't, but that's the only thing I could think of to say."

A black SUV emerged from the Tower's underground parking.

Levack pulled out his cell phone. The screen showed a map with a red blinking dot in the middle.

The dot was moving.

The SUV turned left and drove north.

"No need to keep them in sight," Solaire said. "They will be extra vigilant after my visit, so they'll sense anything out of the ordinary. All we need to know is where they stop."

"Gotcha."

Levack put the car in gear.

They drove for twenty minutes, weaving through traffic, twisting and turning from street to street.

"They are not using the main roads," Levack said. "They know that if they are being followed, it'll be easier to lose their tail on these streets."

The dot on the map finally stopped.

Levack accelerated and then slowed once he saw the SUV was parked in front of a building.

It was Bank of America.

"You think they are depositing or withdrawing?" Levack asked.

Solaire said nothing, but he kept his focus on the bank.

A short while later, Anthony emerged from the front doors. With him were two other men dressed in black. They were holding large silver cases.

"That's a lot of money to be carrying around," Levack said.

Anthony and the two men got in the SUV. Then they did a 360-degree turn and sped away.

"Let's go," Solaire said.

They spent another forty minutes weaving through traffic, but this time they kept to the main roads.

"Where are they going?" Levack asked.

"I think New York Harbor," Solaire replied.

They were soon confronted with rows and rows of shipping containers.

"I should have guessed," Solaire said.

"What?"

"This is where I was brought and roughed up by Fox's goons."

"I could've told you that," Levack said.

Solaire eyed him and then remembered that Levack had put a tracking device on him first.

They drove up carefully.

By now, the sun had started to set.

"There are hundreds of them," Levack said.

"My guess would be in the thousands," Solaire said.

Levack kept one eye on the wheel and the other on the cell phone.

"Looks like they are still moving."

They drove deeper into the harbor, passing the giant metal containers.

"Okay, they've stopped," Levack said. "My guess is they are not too far up ahead."

"Park on the side," Solaire said. "We're walking."

They jogged along the tall rows of containers.

"We should split up," Solaire said.

Levack nodded.

He went down another path while Solaire moved further ahead.

Twenty yards in, Solaire heard noises.

He paused and listened.

They were coming from up ahead.

He peeked from behind a container.

Two vehicles were parked in the middle. One was the black SUV, and the other a gray Mercedes.

Men were unloading the silver cases from the SUV.

Anthony was talking to another person.

Solaire couldn't see who it was. His view was obstructed by the SUV.

He was thinking about changing positions when something cold touched his neck.

He looked up.

A man in a suit was aiming a submachine gun at him.

*Damn*, Solaire thought.

***

As he was marched to the SUV, he recognized the other person.

It was the red-haired man.

The man did not smile. Instead, his eyes filled with venom.

"Get down on your knees," the man with the submachine gun said.

Solaire did as he was told.

The man approached him. "You should have taken my advice and left New York, Mr. Solaire."

"I hadn't seen all the sights yet. The harbor was my last stop. Now that I have seen it, I'll be leaving."

The man finally smiled. "This time, you won't be going anywhere."

Solaire had a feeling the man was more interested in continuing the beating he had inflicted upon him earlier.

Suddenly, the door of the Mercedes opened.

Jackie Belafonte appeared.

She looked as stunning as ever. Her olive skin glowed in the light. Her jet-black hair flowed down to her shoulders.

She walked up to Solaire. Her dark eyes sparkled.

"You don't look surprised to see me, Mr. Solaire," she said, smiling.

"I knew I had made a mistake somewhere."

"And what was that mistake?"

"Failing to realize the target wasn't Guy Fox, but *you*."

"You thought my husband was involved in this?" She laughed. "My husband is a businessman. He cares only for me and money."

"What do you care for?"

"I care for my people."

Solaire was confused.

"If you haven't guessed, I'm half African. My father was born in the Republic of Congo, my mother in Ohio, while I was born in this very city."

"How nice," Solaire said.

Her face remained placid. "I have family all over Africa, which means I have a lot invested. There are those who want to bring democracy to the African region. Democracy is just not possible, Mr. Solaire," she said. "People want democracy, but they don't know how to maintain it. Only people with iron fists can control the population, and my job is to make sure that these people are fully supported."

"You mean, pay for dictators and their militia to kill innocent people."

Jackie scowled. "Like everyone, you are also foolish. There is no such thing as a pure democracy. Even the Western countries that strive for democracy are corrupt themselves. Look at the rich and see how much influence they have on their own government. It is all about self-interest. Why a country invades one country and not the other. Why money is sent to one country and not to the other. Why one country's interests are supported and not the other. It is all about what we get in return and who is giving it."

"I'm not an expert on international relations or even foreign diplomacy," Solaire said, "but sending money to individuals who will use it to buy weapons to massacre innocent people sounds like a crime against humanity. There's no other way of looking at it, no matter how you sugar-coat it."

Jackie did not say anything. Her stare bore into him. Then she said, "You will never understand."

She turned away.

Solaire asked, "Why use your charity?"

She faced him. "It's not easily traceable. In today's electronic world, there's no way to transfer money without leaving a trail. I'm sure that's how you found us. Cash, on the other hand, can disappear. The charity allows us to deliver this cash to those that require it."

"I'm sure the poor and less fortunate could use it more."

Jackie smiled. "I'm sure they could."

"Was it you who had the British agent killed?" Solaire asked.

"Yes. He was getting too close."

"Your husband isn't aware of your involvement in his death?"

"No, he loves me too much to even consider I'm capable of that. I'm capable of much worse." The look in her eyes revealed that she was. "The first time you got off lucky, Mr. Solaire, but now your luck has come to an end."

She motioned to the red-haired man, who cracked his knuckles. He was ready for more fun at Solaire's expense.

"No," she said. "End it quick."

He pulled a gun from behind his back and aimed it directly at Solaire's head.

"Goodbye, Mr. Solaire," Jackie Belafonte said.

***

Solaire prepared himself for the end.

He heard a noise.

He turned toward the sound. They all did.

A Pontiac Sunfire roared at them at high speed.

Jackie's goons fired. Hails of bullets ripped through the windshield, tore into the doors, and shattered the side-view mirrors. But the vehicle did not slow down.

The Pontiac smashed into the SUV like a runaway train.

The impact was deafening. The SUV flipped onto its side, the Pontiac thrusting it forward.

Along the way, it clipped the Mercedes, spinning it 180 degrees, and then the SUV rolled twice before coming to a halt twenty feet away.

Everything happened in an instant.

Solaire couldn't believe what he had just seen.

Suddenly, there was a smell.

He knew what the odor was.

Gas gushed out of the SUV as it lay upside down.

Before anyone could do anything, the SUV and Pontiac exploded.

The power of the blast threw Solaire ten feet in the air.

He landed hard on the ground.

A door from the SUV flew over him and cut into a metal container.

Flames rose up into the sky.

Solaire's face burned from the intense heat.

His hands and knees were badly scraped.

Skin was torn off his knuckles.

He looked around. Everyone was scattered on the ground.

This was his chance.

He got on his feet.

His knees stung, but he ran.

Darkness had fallen, making visibility poor.

Solaire pushed forward.

When he felt he was a good distance away, he stopped to catch his breath.

He looked back. The fire had subsided, leaving a cloud of smoke.

He shook his head. He had come here for a reason: to gather evidence. He couldn't leave without it.

Against his better judgment, Solaire turned and headed back.

He approached the scene of the explosion and carefully surveyed the destruction.

Pieces of the burned SUV lay scattered everywhere.

The Pontiac stood to one side, its front completely crushed in.

The Mercedes was gone, and so were the guards and Jackie Belafonte.

Solaire headed for the first open shipping container.

Barrels were piled inside.

Solaire picked up a crowbar and snapped open the lid of one of the barrels.

Inside were cans of non-perishable food.

He grabbed a can of corn and cut it open with the crowbar's edge.

He drained the can's contents and found a small plastic bag in it.

The bag contained rolled-up hundred-dollar bills.

Solaire pried open the next container.

This one had clothes stuffed in it.

Solaire pulled out a hoodie and felt it.

There was a tiny bulge inside the hood.

He examined the hood. A patch had been sewn into it.

Solaire tore the patch and out came more hundred-dollar bills.

Solaire removed Travers' cell phone and quickly took photos of both the can and the hooded shirt.

He then proceeded to take more photos—the barrels, the contents inside them, and then the entire shipping container.

When he was certain he had enough evidence, he placed the phone back inside his pocket.

He exited the container.

Something hit him hard across the chest.

***

Solaire fell to the ground, clutching his chest.

He looked up.

It was the red-haired man.

"I should have killed you when I had the chance," the man said as he paced around him. "Now, I will."

He kicked Solaire in the stomach.

Solaire grimaced.

"I don't know who you are, but you have caused us a lot of trouble."

He swung his leg again, but this time Solaire blocked it and countered with a kick to the man's shins.

The man howled in pain.

Solaire was on his feet in an instant.

He jabbed his fist at the man's face, connecting with his nose.

Blood flowed from the man's mouth and down his chin.

"This time my hands aren't tied," Solaire said.

The man tried to swing back, but his fist only hit air.

Solaire clutched the man's wrist and twisted it hard.

There was a crack.

Bones snapped.

The man cursed.

Solaire kicked the red-haired man's legs from underneath him.

The man lay on his stomach, writhing and holding his hand.

He tried to crawl away, but Solaire hovered over him.

When Solaire turned him over, he didn't realize the man was holding a piece of metal from the SUV.

The red-haired man swung the metal piece hard, connecting with Solaire's forehead.

Solaire stumbled back.

He shook his head and saw the man crawling in another direction.

Solaire realized why.

A gun lay to one side.

When the explosion had occurred, the impact must have forced the gun out of the man's hand.

Solaire raced after him, but he was too late. The man grabbed the gun, turned, and fired in Solaire's direction.

Solaire ducked and rolled, and in one motion, he grabbed the crowbar and threw it at the man.

The crowbar spun in the air and lodged in the red-haired man's arm.

He screamed.

The gun dropped from his hand.

Solaire dashed over and retrieved the gun.

The red-haired man was clutching his arm, thrashing in pain.

Solaire got on top of him and punched him several times in the face.

The man was covered in cuts and bruises.

"Now, you know how it feels to have your face pummeled," Solaire said.

The red-haired man had nothing but contempt for him.

Solaire aimed the gun between the man's eyes.

He tightened his grip on the butt, his finger on the trigger.

Every fiber in his body was saying *pull it*. He had endured so much, and now he wanted to end it.

But then his body eased, and he relaxed.

"I don't kill," Solaire said. "It's not my style."

Solaire left the red-haired man lying on the ground.

***

The red-haired man watched Solaire disappear into the shadows.

He would go after him, he knew. He would find Roman Solaire, and he would kill him.

He got on his feet.

He pulled the edge of the crowbar out of his arm and hurled it far.

He spat blood.

Solaire had made a huge mistake. A mistake he would regret.

He heard a noise.

He turned.

A figure emerged from the shadows.

Before the man could say anything, two gunshots were fired. The first bullet tore through the red-haired man's chest. The second went straight between his eyes.

The man fell to the ground like a rag doll.

Donald Levack put the gun back inside his jacket.

"I *do* kill," he said. "It *is* my style."

***

Solaire unlocked the door to his room and entered.

He was battered and bruised, but he didn't care. It was over.

He turned the lights on and stopped.

Seated near the balcony doors was Travers.

"Why am I not surprised to see you?" Solaire said.

He walked straight to the bathroom.

He cleaned himself up and came out.

Travers said, "I spoke to Levack, and he told me how the money was being smuggled across the ocean."

Solaire pulled out the cell phone and threw it in Travers' direction.

Traver's caught the phone. "It's all in here?" he asked.

Solaire nodded and sat on the edge of the bed.

"We were certain Guy Fox was involved, but never in a million years did we suspect his wife," Travers said.

"Well, it could have saved me a lot of trouble," Solaire shot back.

"I'm being honest with you," Travers said. "If we had known that, then the British agent would still be alive now."

"You don't seem too upset by his death."

"I did send Levack to protect you."

"You sent him so I could finish the job," Solaire retorted. "You were protecting your asset. Isn't that what I am to you? What is it that you said… 'Use the asset to complete the mission?'"

Travers said nothing.

"Well, the mission is complete. What now?"

Travers pulled out a manila envelope from his coat and placed it on the bed.

Solaire knew the folder contained the photos of his work in Toronto.

"They are all there," Travers said. "The originals were destroyed."

"I'll take your word for it," Solaire said, but he wasn't convinced.

"I never intended to blackmail you, Roman."

"Are we on a first-name basis now?" Solaire said. "And what should I call you?"

Travers paused and then said, "It's Clive. Clive Travers."

"Nice to meet you, Clive," Solaire said half-heartedly.

"I guarantee you that even if you weren't able to complete the mission, those photos would never have been seen by another person."

Solaire stared at him. It looked like Travers was sincere—or he was a very good liar.

"What you did tonight," Travers said, "you have no idea how much good it will do for the world."

"Is that what I'm doing?" Solaire asked. "Saving the world? The last time I checked, I was posing as someone else, lying to people, breaking into homes, and beating people up."

"A necessary evil, I assure you."

"I'm sure it is."

Travers uncrossed his legs. "I think I owe you an explanation."

"It would be nice." Solaire touched his forehead, feeling the spot where the red-haired man had hit him earlier.

"Have you heard of CIL?" Travers asked.

Solaire shook his head.

"The Court of International Law. Our mandate is to prosecute those who affect international stability."

Solaire was intrigued. "Okay."

"We are an international governing body fully supported by the United Nations. For months now, we have been trying to find evidence against Guy Fox, which we now know, was incorrect. A grave and severe error on our part, I concede. The international community has been closely watching us. We have tried, and failed, on numerous occasions to prosecute war criminals, dictators, government leaders, all those that affect peace and harmony in the world."

"Jackie Belafonte is none of those," Solaire said.

"Yes, but she was funding state terrorism. Thanks to your help, we now have enough evidence to prosecute her and those she was providing money to."

"They are just photos," Solaire said.

"Yes, but they provide us with information on how the operation worked. Right now, as I speak, with the help of the local authorities, we have those shipping containers secured. Roman…" Travers paused for a second. "There are countries, including the United States, that do not want their citizens prosecuted in a foreign court, even if that court is recognized by the United Nations."

"What you are saying is that Jackie Belafonte will not be charged?"

"No, she will be. The new administration is willing to recognize CIL, if CIL completes its mandate with care."

"I don't think anything I did would be considered *completing with care*."

Travers smiled. "That is why no one will ever know that you work for CIL."

"Who said I do?"

"I'm hoping you would consider it."

Solaire thought for a moment. "Does Levack work for you?"

"Not directly. Let's just say, he's a hired consultant."

"And what would I be?"

"An advisor."

Solaire finally laughed. "You people have a way with words."

"Are you interested in assisting in the capture of international criminals?"

Solaire got up from the bed. "I'll think about it," he said. "Right now, I think my mind and my body could use a bit of rest."

"Right."

Travers nodded and stood up.

Solaire said, "What about the money? I may have spent it all."

"CIL has no problems when it comes to money. In fact, we can provide it to you in any denomination you like."

"Does CIL have its own credit card?"

"I'm afraid not."

"Cash only?"

"I'm afraid so."

Solaire understood.

"Goodnight, Mr. Roman Solaire," Travers said. "I hope you will consider my offer. Your services will be a benefit to people all over."

Solaire watched the door close.

He dropped back on the bed.

His head was pounding not only from the beating he had taken earlier but also from what Travers had just said.

He turned the lights off and instantly fell asleep.

***

The next day, Solaire lay in bed in his hotel room. He ordered breakfast: fresh fruits, scrambled eggs, a glass of orange juice, and a cup of steaming tea. Lunch consisted of chilled cucumber soup, a light salad, and a pan-roasted halibut with rice.

He spent the time watching the news.

There was a brief story of a raid at New York Harbor, but no mention of anything specific.

If Travers was telling the truth, then more details would come to light in the coming days.

There was a news item, though, that caught Solaire's attention.

A dead body was found at the harbor.

They described him as a male with red hair.

Solaire was certain the red-haired man was alive and breathing when he had left him.

But Solaire had a hunch.

He took two more painkillers and went back to bed.

Late that afternoon, Solaire strolled out into the New York streets.

He didn't know if it was safe to be out and about. What if Guy Fox's goons came after him?

He didn't care.

He had spent too much time in New York working and not enough time enjoying its sights and sounds.

He walked over to Rizzuto & Sons. He returned Crystal Towers' master key and gave Mario a thick envelope of money. Travers wouldn't miss any of it.

He then stopped at a restaurant and ordered an iced tea.

When he was halfway through his drink, a man came over and sat down at his table.

"Iced tea with no ice?" Donald Levack inquired.

Solaire nodded.

"Heck, why not?" he said and ordered one just like Solaire.

He took a sip and licked his lips.

"I see why you do that," he said. "The ice dilutes the taste."

"They found a dead body at the harbor. Any idea why that might be?" Solaire asked.

Levack shook his head. "I wouldn't know. After we split up, I got tired of walking around the shipping containers, so I went home. I was able to catch the second half of the Knicks versus the Lakers. Great game. It came down to the wire."

"And you wouldn't have any idea how a Pontiac Sunfire plowed into an SUV, would you?"

"Really?" Levack looked shocked. "That must have been dangerous. Glad I wasn't around to see that."

Solaire finally laughed. "Where are you off to now?"

"I don't know." Levack shrugged. "Haven't got my orders yet. What about you?"

"I haven't decided."

Levack slurped more of his tea. "Maybe we could work on the next one together."

Solaire looked at Levack. He was serious.

"Hey," Levack said. "In my line of work, you don't make too many friends, at least not friends who live long enough to become annoying."

Solaire stared at him. This time he saw Levack wasn't serious.

"Thank you for saving my life," Solaire said.

Levack finished his drink and got up. "I don't do man hugs."

Levack held his hand out.

Solaire shook it.

"Maybe I'll see you again," Levack said. "In another city, perhaps."

Solaire didn't know what that meant, but he said, "Perhaps."

He watched Levack walk down the street.

***

Solaire waited outside with his hands in his pockets. The air had gotten unusually chilly as night fell.

He watched a few people come in and out of the building.

When she came out, he smiled.

"I didn't think I'd see you," Sandy said.

"Why not?" he asked.

"I don't know. I just had a feeling."

"Well, you were wrong, and I am here."

She smiled. "Okay."

"I was thinking," Solaire said. "Why don't I take you to a Broadway show?"

Sandy eyed him.

"Listen," he said. "I can't leave New York without at least seeing one show. What's the point in coming all the way here?"

"You're leaving?"

Sandy seemed disappointed.

"My flight's tonight."

"You can't stay?"

He shook his head. "I've got my orders. So, Ms. Sandy Williams, would you like to take Mr. Roman Solaire out on the town?"

"Yes."

She smiled and put her arm around his.

***

After watching the musical, they walked down the bustling, brightly lit street.

Solaire was now convinced New York City was indeed the one place where no one slept.

"Where's home?" Sandy asked.

He considered whether to tell her or not, but then he replied, "Toronto."

"You're Canadian? I'm not surprised."

"Why would you say that?"

"You're too nice."

"I'm not as nice as you think I am."

She smiled at him. "You're nice to me."

They continued walking.

"Did you get in trouble for the list?" Solaire asked.

"No, Patrick has no idea it was missing. Did it help?"

"In more ways than you think."

She stopped. "There was something odd I heard today. Some murmurs about Jackie Belafonte. Did you have anything to do with that?"

Solaire put his hands up. "I plead the fifth."

"You can't plead the fifth. You're not an American."

"Then, I plead innocence."

Sandy stared at him. "You *are* dangerous, Mr. Solaire. Very dangerous."

"Guilty as charged."

They continued walking and then stopped in front of a building.

"My place," she said.

"You still enjoy working at the real estate agency?" Solaire asked.

"What can a girl do?" Sandy shrugged. "I've got rent to pay."

Solaire put his hand inside his jacket and pulled out an envelope.

"What's this?" she asked.

"Take it."

She opened the envelope. Inside was a card. It read, *Go live your dream. Be a star on Broadway!*

The envelope was filled with hundred-dollar bills.

"That's a lot of money," she said.

"My way of saying thanks," he said.

"I don't know," she said.

"Do you want to keep working for Patrick?" he asked.

Sandy thought for a moment and then kissed him on the cheek.

A second later, she kissed him on the mouth—a parting kiss, which Solaire returned.

"Good night, Ms. Williams," he said with a bow.

"Good night, Mr. Solaire," she said.

*****

Solaire went back to the Ritz-Carlton.

He packed his bag and then waited by the hotel door.

A familiar taxi halted.

Jagjit Singh emerged, smiling.

He placed Solaire's carry-on in the trunk, and they drove off.

Jag had a million questions regarding Solaire's visit to New York.

Solaire politely answered all of them, without giving any details.

They reached JFK International Airport.

Jag quickly retrieved Solaire's carry-on.

"Will you come back to New York?" Jag asked.

"I think I will, but next time it won't be for business," Solaire replied.

## The Royal Bank of Lords

THE HAGUE

"The mission in New York was a success," the Englishman said.

Travers, seated across from him, didn't respond.

The Dutchman said, "The information you provided has given our organization serious credibility in the international community."

The man only smiled.

"Who is this man of yours?" the Englishman asked.

"I can't say," Travers replied.

"Why not?" the Dutchman fumed.

"It is better that it be kept that way for now."

The Englishman stared hard at Travers. "Our organization is putting a lot of money into this…"

"And we have delivered," Travers quickly interjected.

"Yes, but it would be nice to know where that money is going."

Travers leaned forward. "It is going exactly where it should be. What happened in New York is proof of that."

The Englishman looked at the Dutchman.

The Dutchman nodded.

"Where is your man now?" the Englishman asked Travers.

"In London."

LONDON

Roman Solaire sat near the fountain and watched the tourists snap photos of it.

Trafalgar Square, located in central London, was much cleaner now than when he had visited it many years ago.

Perhaps it was the pigeons or lack thereof. He remembered there used to be thousands of them all over the square like locusts, and they left a mess behind. The problem caused by their droppings was so bad that it became a health hazard. It wasn't until it became illegal to feed the pigeons that the square was able to be rid of them.

Solaire squinted at the center of the square, particularly at Nelson's Column, which was surrounded by four statues of lions.

He felt someone sit next to him.

"I was beginning to wonder when you would show up," Solaire said, not looking away from the column.

"I thought I would give you some time to recover from your last mission," Clive Travers said.

"That was very kind of you," Solaire said, without a hint of a compliment.

Travers was beginning to get used to Solaire's pointed remarks.

"There must be a reason why I'm here," Solaire said, finally looking at him.

"Yes, there is."

Travers pulled out a yellow envelope.

Inside were black and white photographs of three people.

"You do know we are in the twenty-first century," Solaire said.

"Have you heard of the Royal Bank of Lords, or RBL?" Travers asked, ignoring Solaire's remark.

Solaire shook his head.

"RBL was created during World War II by a group of wealthy individuals. They wanted to protect their money from the British government. While the country sacrificed their health and wealth to win the war, these individuals only built upon their investments. There were rumors the bank was used to funnel Nazi money. This, however, cannot be substantiated."

"Why didn't the government go after them?"

"The patrons of RBL went as high up as the royal family."

"The Queen?" Solaire inquired.

"Not that high up. Plus, after the war, the government needed investors to help rebuild the country. RBL was more than glad to. They acquired land at cutthroat prices and built businesses on them. Those businesses generated jobs and money for the government, so no one really complained." Travers glanced at the tourists gathered in the square. "RBL was only open to private and privileged investors."

"You mean the rich?" Solaire asked.

"The super-rich," Travers answered. "No less than one million dollars was required to open an account."

"That's double what most Swiss banks require," Solaire said.

"Yes, and they didn't mind who invested. Dictators, oil barons, sheiks, warlords—if you had money, you were welcomed with open arms."

Solaire made a face. "You want me to find out where they are hiding their dirty money?"

"No, we already know."

Solaire was confused.

"Then in the mid-eighties," Travers said, "RBL opened their doors to everyone, not just to the privileged few. It no longer required the initial million-dollar deposit. Money poured in at RBL during the nineties. Investors from all over opened accounts. People on salaries and pensions, small and medium businesses, large and small corporations, all came rushing in with their cash. It seemed that RBL had finally become legitimate until the millennium rolled around. They began making risky investments, and by the end of the last decade, when the recession hit, they had lost close to a trillion dollars."

Solaire waited for more.

"Those individuals in the photographs are board members of RBL," Travers said.

Solaire held the first one up. The man in the photo was clean-shaven with a receding hairline.

"Sir Anthony Blairwood," Travers said.

Solaire looked at the next photo. It was of a woman. She was older, and she had hair that resembled a bird's nest.

"Lady Marge Thatchburn."

Solaire held up the last photo. The man in the picture was heavyset with graying hair.

"Lord Cornell Blacksmith."

"They all have titles?" Solaire asked.

"And why wouldn't they?" Travers replied. "Before the recession, RBL was the crown jewel in England's banking circles."

"What's special about them?" Solaire asked, glancing at the photos again.

"While the average person has lost his or her entire life's savings, RBL has only increased their net worth, making millions of pounds during the financial meltdown." Travers pulled out another photo. This one was in color. The man in the photo was middle-aged, and he wore glasses. "Robbie Fisk," Travers said. "He was another member of the board."

"No title?" Solaire inquired.

"He became a board member only a few years ago, so I guess that was not long enough for any honors. Fisk's car was found in the Thames. It may have been a suicide, but no suicide note was found, and his body has not been found, either."

Solaire looked into the distance.

"Prior to his disappearance, Fisk's behavior had become strange. He looked worried and under stress. Some said they had spotted him with a younger woman, so he may have been having an affair. But that's not of our concern. What we are interested in is that Fisk may have left incriminating evidence against the other board members. Find it so we can prosecute them."

"Why?" Solaire asked, turning to Travers.

"What do you mean?"

"Why is CIL going after board members of a bank?"

"The Court of International Law's mandate is to prosecute those that affect international stability. Investors from all over had invested in RBL. The one trillion lost has had a ripple effect globally. It has destabilized markets throughout many countries."

Solaire squinted, as if in deep thought.

"Roman," Travers said. "These people may dress in business suits, but they are still criminals. W—I mean, you—have to bring them before the international court so they can be charged for these crimes."

"There are many financial institutions around the world that are doing exactly what they have done, so why go after them?"

"The British people are outraged by what has happened, so the British government is allowing us to make an example of them. If we are successful, then other countries may follow suit."

Solaire stared at the photos of Blairwood, Thatchburn, and Blacksmith.

"All right," he finally said.

***

Solaire took the tube to St. John's Wood Station. From there, he walked the two blocks to St. John's Wood High Street, where he had rented an apartment for a week. He could have gone to a swanky hotel, but this time he wanted to stay low-key. His flat was on the top floor, but instead of taking the elevator, he took the stairs.

The apartment was bare and not at all luxurious. Solaire wasn't overly concerned, though. He wouldn't be spending too much time there anyway.

He turned his laptop on and placed the phone Travers had given him next to it.

He spent the next several hours researching RBL and its board members.

As darkness was falling, he left his flat.

Outside, the air was much cooler.

London at night was as vibrant as it was in the morning.

A group of five people came out of one of the pubs, laughing and sounding a little too excited.

Solaire decided to go in.

The pub's lights were low-lit, giving it a feeling of coziness.

Solaire was surprised to see the number of people inside. It was a weekday, after all.

*The Brits love their pubs*, Solaire thought, remembering something he was once told.

He went up to the bar.

"What can I get ya?" the barman said.

"Do you have iced tea?" Solaire asked.

The barman made a face. "This is a pub, mate. You wanna get tipsy, then you come here, if you know what I mean."

Solaire nodded.

He was about to leave when the barman asked, "You an American?"

"Canadian," Solaire replied.

The barman smiled. "Welcome to London, mate. Wait here."

The barman disappeared in the back.

Solaire looked around.

The patrons consisted of people, young and old.

The barman returned with an orange bottle of soda that bore the name *Fanta*.

He unscrewed the cap and placed it in front of Solaire.

"Can't have you leaving here without a drink," the barman said.

Solaire took a sip. It was a fruit-flavored soft drink.

The barman smiled. "I keep a bottle or two in the back for when we get kids in the pub."

"Yeah, I guess that would be me."

Solaire smiled and took another sip.

"The name's Martin Humphries," the barman said, extending his hand.

"Roman Solaire."

Humphries had a face akin to a hound dog. His cheeks, ears, and even eyes drooped. But there was a hint of kindness in his blue eyes.

"Where in Canada are you from?" Humphries asked.

"Toronto."

"Oh, I've got a cousin who lives there. His name is Chris…"

"Toronto is a big city," Solaire quickly said, knowing where this was going.

"Right," Humphries said, quickly understanding Solaire was not interested in chit-chat. "Let me know if you need anything else."

He walked away.

Solaire looked at the TV perched high up.

A football game was on. Arsenal was up two-one to Manchester United.

Solaire had never been a sports fan. He was, though, conscious of all the sports—baseball, basketball, hockey, and even cricket. He understood their rules and regulations. But he was not the type to spend his afternoons or evenings glued to the television watching a game.

Humphries returned. "Can I get you another?"

Solaire looked at his half-empty bottle and shook his head. "Tell me," he said. "If I were looking for information in London, where would I start?"

"It depends."

"On what?"

"What type of information you are looking for."

"Information on a certain bank. The Royal Bank of Lords, to be specific."

"You lose money in that bank?"

"You can say that."

Humphries shook his head. "Sorry, can't help you there."

Solaire nodded and got up. "How much do I owe you for the…" he checked the name on the bottle, "Fanta?"

"It's on the house. I don't usually charge the little ones for a drink."

Humphries smiled.

***

The next morning, Solaire took the tube to RBL's headquarters in Central London. Solaire could see the building was huge, made of concrete and granite. Near the entrance, a small group of people were gathered around.

A woman was standing in the front and shouting something.

Solaire got closer.

"They should be locked up," the woman said.

Solaire noticed the crowd was holding handmade posters of Blairwood, Thatchburn, and Blacksmith. The posters weren't flattering, to say the least.

"They are nothing but crooks!" the woman yelled. "They lost our money, and the government is doing nothing about it. We want justice! We want our money!"

The crowd yelled back approvingly, waving their signs with defiance.

Suddenly, a police vehicle pulled up and ordered the crowd away.

Solaire waited.

A man in a suit emerged from the building and spoke a few words with the police officers.

The man looked to his left and to his right, and then he went inside.

Solaire approached the doorman.

"Excuse me," Solaire said. "Can you tell me who that person was that just went inside?"

The doorman looked Solaire up and down. "Why do you want to know?"

Solaire pulled out a hundred-pound note. "He dropped it on the side of the road, and I wanted to return it."

"I'll give it to him," the doorman said.

"I don't know," Solaire said, making it sound like he was unsure.

"Mr. David Clampton is a very busy man. I would hate to disturb him." The doorman's eyes never left the note.

"All right," Solaire said. He held the hundred-pound note for the doorman, who quickly snatched it. "Please make sure he gets it."

"I will."

***

Solaire went into an internet café and quickly did a search on Clampton. David Clampton had been an employee of RBL for eleven years. He had started off as the personal bodyguard to Lady Thatchburn, and from there, he moved all the way up to RBL's head of security.

Solaire looked at his watch. It was almost noon.

He stood across the street from RBL's headquarters.

Solaire spotted a group of people coming out. They were dressed in business suits and other professional attire. They were obviously headed out for lunch.

Solaire kept waiting.

Almost half an hour later, David Clampton came out of the building.

He pulled out a cigarette, lit it, and began puffing away.

Solaire followed behind.

Clampton walked down the block, turned right, and kept walking.

He stopped in front of a restaurant, put his cigarette out, and went in.

Solaire went in too.

Inside, Clampton sat at the back of the restaurant.

The maître d placed Solaire a few tables from Clampton.

Solaire looked at the menu. The prices were something he could never afford on his own. Luckily, money was never an issue for his employers.

He ordered what looked like halibut with rice, along with some greens on the side.

*I don't get why restaurants use foreign words to describe their dishes*, he thought after the waiter left.

He surreptitiously watched Clampton devour his appetizers.

Clampton's thinning hair was slicked back. His suit was tight on his body, exposing his protruding belly, so much so that it looked as if his shirt buttons were ready to pop. He wore a gold ring on his left pinky finger.

Solaire's order came.

He slowly bit into the halibut. It was far more delicious than he anticipated. *Maybe the meal was worth the price*, he thought.

Exactly an hour later, Clampton got up and left the restaurant.

Solaire paid the bill and followed.

Clampton walked back to RBL and then disappeared inside.

Solaire looked at his watch. He now knew Clampton's afternoon schedule.

***

Solaire hailed a cab and gave the driver directions.

He watched the London streets pass by.

He was not surprised by how busy they were.

The very first time he had visited London, he had come to appreciate that.

Solaire still clearly remembered sightseeing in the city. He had been amazed at seeing people from all over the globe freely interacting with one another.

He had seen people from Asia, Africa, Scandinavia, the Middle East, and other parts of Europe on the same train. He was awed at all the different languages that were being spoken at one time.

He had become convinced that London was a melting pot of cultures.

Like New York, his previous destination, London was also a city that never slept.

Tourists from all over poured into the city to see all the attractions it had to offer.

Every nook and cranny of the city was filled with some historical significance. He remembered standing in front of a house where Mahatma Gandhi had once lived when he was a law student. And today, the cab took him by several more locations the city had deemed heritage sites.

The driver dropped him off in Kensington.

The white row of houses went all the way down the street.

Each house was so attached to the other that a passerby could mistake them as part of one complete building.

Solaire pulled out a business card, which he had used on other assignments, and moved his fingers over the lettering.

He approached the door and rang the bell.

A few seconds later, the door opened. A gray-haired woman said, "Can I help you?"

"Yes." Solaire smiled. "Is Mrs. Fisk at home?"

The woman examined Solaire up and down. He was casually dressed—brown khaki pants, a white dress shirt, and a blue jacket.

Solaire gave her his best smile.

"May I know who's looking for her?" the woman asked.

Solaire handed her the card.

The woman looked at it.

"Can you give it to her, please?" he said, still smiling.

The woman looked at him, nodded, and shut the door.

He waited.

The street was quiet save for a couple of cars driving by. Solaire noticed that all the cars in the neighborhood were luxurious. He spotted a BMW, a Mercedes Benz, and even a Bentley.

The door opened again.

"How can I help you…?" a young woman asked. She glanced at the card. "Mr. Bind."

"Jim Bind." Solaire smiled.

"Yes."

"Can we talk inside?"

The woman hesitated.

Solaire said, "Mrs. Fisk, as you can tell from the card, I am a private investigator. I was hired to find your husband."

Mrs. Fisk was taken aback. "Is this some kind of joke?"

"I assure you this is no joke."

Tears formed in her eyes. "I'm not sure if you know, but my husband committed suicide."

"I am aware of this."

"Then why would you disturb a grieving widow?"

"I have no desire to cause any undue stress, ma'am. I am only here to make certain that what was reported is the case."

Mrs. Fisk bit her lip.

Solaire added, "As you can tell from my accent, I'm not from here. I came all the way from Canada. I only want to ask a few questions, and then you'll never see me again."

She held the door for him. "Please come in."

***

The room was opulent. The floor was hardwood with an embroidered Persian rug on top of it. The ceilings went high up with natural light coming down from expansive windows. The walls were white and bare. There was an unused fireplace with a shelf above it. Family photos covered the shelf.

Solaire spotted Fisk in many of the photos. In some, he was smiling with his wife and two sons, while in others, he was standing in front of buildings and other properties.

"He was so proud of those," Mrs. Fisk said, pointing to one of the photos.

They were in the middle of the room, sitting on large leather sofas.

Mrs. Fisk wore a light green dress that was knee-length. Her dark hair was shoulder length. Her skin was pale but radiant. She looked much younger than her age. The only thing out of the ordinary was the bags underneath her eyes, a mute testimony to the grief and strain she had been enduring.

"He genuinely believed the bank was helping regular people," Mrs. Fisk continued. "He thought that by approving so many loans, he was empowering people to become homeowners or business owners." She fell silent. "Robbie didn't come from a wealthy family. In fact, growing up, he was even lower than what you would call middle class. His father worked at a factory that made buttons, and his mother cleaned people's houses. I, on the other hand, was lucky to have grown up in affluence. My father was a member of parliament, and my mother ran a successful clothing line."

The gray-haired woman entered the room, holding a tray. She gently placed it on the table before them.

"Would you like me to pour it, sir?" she asked.

"No, I am fine. Thank you," Solaire replied.

She turned to Mrs. Fisk. "Ma'am?"

"No, maybe later. Thank you."

The woman left the room.

Mrs. Fisk resumed speaking. "Robbie worked hard and borrowed money to pay for his education. He was smart enough to get into Oxford. That's where I met him." She smiled, but it was tinged with sadness. "He was unlike anyone I had ever met. You have to realize that growing up in the environment that I did, everything was—how do I say it? Sheltered. Robbie was without any constraints. Being with him, I felt alive. There were no such things as what was proper for me, or what was expected of me, or what my future held. With Robbie the future held endless possibilities, and we were free to pursue any of them. As you can imagine, my parents weren't too happy when we decided to get married. They were ready to cut me off, but Robbie was able to win them over. He always had a way with people. He brought out the best in them. Anyway, the first couple of years were trying, to say the least. Robbie refused to take help from my parents. He was too proud. He started as a broker in a small investment firm and worked his way…" She stopped, her eyes glinting with hurt. "He became a board member of the Royal Bank of Lords."

Solaire carefully asked, "Mrs. Fisk, was your husband happy at RBL?"

She thought for a moment. "He was, at first. I mean, who wouldn't be? The pay, along with prestige, was too much to turn away. Just the signing bonus paid for this house." She motioned around the room. "I did, however, notice his behavior change in the last couple of months."

"How so?"

"I mean, he became quieter, more reserved. I knew he was under a lot of stress. I'm sure you heard of what happened at the bank?"

Solaire nodded.

"But there was something else."

Mrs. Fisk fell silent.

"You mean the other woman?" Solaire said.

She bit her lip in order to control her emotions.

"I'm sorry if this is hard, Mrs. Fisk."

She shook her head. "I don't believe it," she said.

He waited for her to continue.

"Robbie was a good man. He was also a strong man," she said defiantly. "He would have never strayed from our marriage, and he most certainly would not have killed himself."

"Can you tell me anything that might help me find him?" Solaire said. "Did he have any enemies?"

She laughed. "Sure, he did. Anyone who had invested in the bank despised him. They blamed him for what happened to them, even though he had no idea what was going on in the bank. It was those *three* who were behind it."

Solaire knew she was referring to Blairwood, Thatchburn, and Blacksmith.

"If you want to find out more, you should talk to them," she said.

"I'm going to try."

Mrs. Fisk was quiet.

Solaire knew it was his cue to leave.

"Thank you for your time, Mrs. Fisk." He got up.

"I wish I could have been of more help to you," she said.

"You have."

He was about to leave when he spotted something on the side table.

"What is that?" he asked.

She picked it up and handed it to him.

It was an invitation to a party held by RBL.

"It's for their highly-valued investors. The bank hosts it annually. Naturally, I am invited, but under the circumstances, I don't have the heart to go."

"Will the other board members be there?"

"Of course. They are the face of the bank."

"How does one get invited to this event?"

She smiled. "I know what you are thinking, but invitation is highly restricted."

"That's not a problem. I'm resourceful." He smiled.

She eyed him. "Whoever hired you must be paying you well. Can I ask who they are?"

"I'm afraid it's confidential. But I can assure you their intentions are good, or else I wouldn't be working for them."

"I'm glad to hear that." She smiled. "If you are so inclined to be at the event, then I would recommend you speak to Louise Mapother. She is the bank's extra affairs liaison."

"Thank you."

She walked him to the door.

"There was someone else who came asking questions about my husband," she said.

"Can you describe this person?" Solaire asked.

"She was tall, fair skin, blue eyes, and she had long silver hair."

"Silver hair?" Solaire said.

"Yes. I remember it clearly because I said to myself it was an odd choice for hair color."

Solaire thought for a moment and then said, "Thank you, Mrs. Fisk."

***

Instead of taking a taxi, Solaire headed for South Kensington Station.

He stood on the platform. On the way to the station, he had already mapped out his route back to his flat. He would take the Circle Line, interchange at Westminster Station for the Jubilee Line, and take it all the way to St. John's Wood Station.

While waiting for the train, he spotted someone at the other end of the platform.

Solaire couldn't clearly make out the face; the person was too far away. But he could see that the man wore an odd-looking gray coat, with an even odder- looking gray hat.

The man's attire made him look like he didn't belong in the twenty-first Century. Incongruously, though, he also wore dark sunglasses.

But what caught Solaire's attention was the way the man was looking in his direction.

The train approached the platform.

Solaire watched the man.

Not once did he look away.

The train's doors opened, and Solaire entered.

Solaire suddenly had a bad feeling in the pit of his stomach. A sixth sense was warning him that the man was trouble.

The train moved along on its designated route.

It stopped at Sloan Square Station and then continued on.

Solaire glanced at the Underground map.

The train would stop at Victoria Station, St. James's Park Station, and then at Westminster Station, where he was supposed to change lines. But before he could do that, he had to be sure he wasn't being followed.

At St. James's Park Station, Solaire popped his head out of doors. To his horror, the man stood halfway out the doors of his compartment. He could clearly see everyone going in and out of the train.

Solaire went back in.

He was now certain that he was being followed, but by whom?

No one, except for Travers, knew he was in London.

Solaire had enemies from previous missions. *Could this person be one of them?* he thought.

Solaire wasn't waiting to find out.

He watched as the train approached Westminster Station. He didn't dare get off. He couldn't lead this person to his flat. He had to lose him.

Solaire examined the Underground map.

He quickly charted an alternative route.

When the doors opened at Embankment Station, Solaire bolted.

He rushed down the halls, through the stairs, and toward another platform.

At the Bakerloo Line, he waited for the train.

The train approached. Solaire was about to board when he spotted the man. Like before, the man was standing at the other end of the platform.

He was looking in Solaire's direction.

Solaire got on the train.

Solaire was surprised that he had failed to elude the man.

He watched as Charing Cross Station, Piccadilly Circus Station, and Oxford Circus Station passed by.

When he was at Regent's Park Station, Solaire decided that he would make a run for it at the next stop. It was an interchange station, which would be perfect for his getaway.

The train's doors opened at Baker Street Station, and Solaire was the first passenger out.

He rushed down the halls, through the stairs and escalators, and reached the Jubilee Line platform.

He watched and waited for the man to appear down at the other end of the platform. But by the time the train approached, the man was nowhere to be found.

Relieved, Solaire got aboard.

He found a seat and rested his head on the side.

When the train stopped at St. John's Wood Station, Solaire got off.

He stood on the long escalator as it slowly moved up toward the station's entrance.

When he was closer to the top, he spotted something.

The man was standing by the escalator with his hands in his pockets.

Solaire thought about doubling back, but the escalator was too narrow, and there were too many people behind him.

As the escalator slowly took him closer to the man, Solaire hatched a plan.

Just as he was almost to the top, he jumped over the side of the escalator and landed on a flight of stairs.

He rushed up, pushed past the man, and ran toward the exit.

As he was about to reach the doors, a familiar voice said, "Roman, wait!"

Solaire stopped and turned.

***

Donald Levack was putting on his hat and adjusting his coat.

He was middle-aged and slightly overweight with green eyes, which were currently hidden by the sunglasses.

"What are you doing here?" Solaire asked.

Levack shrugged. "I thought I'd sightsee in London, you know?"

Upon closer examination, Solaire realized what Levack was wearing. It was Sherlock Holmes's Deerstalker hat and his long, caped tweed coat.

"Why are you dressed like that?" Solaire asked.

"I thought I'd blend in with the locals."

"Where'd you get it, a costume shop?" Solaire said.

"As a matter of fact," Levack said, mimicking a fake British accent. "I did, old chap."

"I hope you don't have a pipe somewhere in there."

Levack's eyes brightened. "I actually do." He pulled out an S-shaped pipe from inside his coat. "It came with the costume. And look here." He pulled out a large magnifying glass. "We can now go investigating."

"I'm going to ask again," Solaire said. "What are you doing here?"

"It's a free country, last I heard," Levack answered. "Actually, I was thinking of checking out Madame Tussauds. I really want to get a picture with Attila the Hun."

"Okay, then why are you following me?"

"Who said I was following you?"

"I saw you at South Kensington Station and then at Embankment Station. You were following me. It looked as if…" Solaire stopped and then shook his head. "*Travers.* He sent you, didn't he?"

Levack put his hands up. "You got me."

"All right, come. I'll buy you a drink," Solaire finally said. "I know a good place."

***

They entered the pub and went up to the bar.

Humphries looked at them and, without a hint of sarcasm, said, "What're you supposed to be, Sherlock Holmes and his faithful sidekick, Dr. Watson?"

Solaire just sat on the stool.

Humphries leaned over and said with a smile, "You're underdressed for the part, mate."

"I know," Solaire said. "I'll have—

"I've got just the thing for you." Humphries winked. "What about you, Mr. Holmes?" Humphries turned to Levack. "What can I get ya?"

"I'll have your best soda water," Levack replied in his fake British accent.

"You too?" Humphries shook his head and left them.

"How's sobriety coming along?" Solaire asked.

Levack shrugged. "It's coming."

"How long have you been in the city?"

"I flew in last night."

"Did Travers tell you about the mission?"

"Only what was necessary."

"I appreciate you coming here, but I can handle this myself," Solaire said.

"I know, I know," Levack said. "I'll stay in the background. I won't get in your way. Just think of me as your designated *hitter*, if or when things get dicey." Levack pulled his coat open. Solaire spotted a gun in his belt.

"I don't work with guns," Solaire said.

"I know." Levack smiled. "But I do."

Humphries returned with their drinks.

He placed a large glass in front of Levack. "The best soda water in all of London." He then placed another glass in front of Solaire. "Iced tea just for you, mate. I picked it up, knowing you might be back."

Solaire looked at his drink.

"He doesn't like ice in his iced tea," Levack quickly said.

"It's fine." Solaire smiled. "Thank you."

"Right," Humphries said. "I'll leave you two. If you need anything, just whistle."

Solaire sipped his iced tea. It was cool and refreshing.

Levack made a face after sipping his drink. He asked, "Are you making progress?"

"It's coming along," Solaire replied.

"Travers was really impressed with you in New York."

"Was he?"

"He didn't actually say it, but I could tell."

Solaire looked at him.

"What I'm saying is he wouldn't have asked me to come all this way if he didn't think you were valuable."

Solaire took a sip.

"Plus, I don't mind," Levack said. "New York was fun."

"You have a weird sense of fun," Solaire said. "From what I remember, *I* barely made it through."

Levack leaned over. "But you did, and that's why we're here to fight another day."

Solaire didn't know what to say.

"Don't get me wrong," Levack said. "I don't have any morbid fascination with death, but compared to what I did before, this is way more exciting."

Solaire eyed him. "And what is it exactly that you did before?"

Levack hesitated.

Solaire said, "You know more about me than I do about you. That hardly seems fair, considering we are to trust each other with our lives."

Levack thought for a moment. "Okay, let's say I was a pencil-sharpening, paper-pushing, staple-removing kind of guy. The only exhilarating thing I did all day was change the date on the date-stamper."

"That still doesn't tell me anything about you," Solaire said.

"That's all you'll get for today," Levack said.

Humphries came over. "Sorry to interrupt, but there is someone who wants to speak to you, mate." He pointed toward a booth in the corner.

Solaire noticed it was occupied by one person—a young woman.

"Wow, she's cute," Levack said.

"Did she say why?" Solaire asked.

"Who cares," Levack interjected. "I'll go if you don't."

Humphries said, "I think you'll find what she says very interesting."

Solaire got up.

Levack slapped him on the shoulder. "Don't worry. If you need help, I'm right here with my drink."

***

She had short blonde hair, large blue eyes, and a round face. She wore a light jacket, a white blouse, and gray cargo pants.

Solaire slid into the opposite side of the booth. "I was told you wanted to speak to me. I'm Roman Solaire."

"I know who you are," she said. "Martin told me."

Solaire glanced over at Humphries, who was busy with other customers.

"How can I help you, Ms.…?"

"Emma Morgan," she replied.

"Ms. Morgan, how—?"

"Mr. Solaire," she said, and then she paused. "Why are you interested in the Royal Bank of Lords?"

It was Solaire's turn to pause. "I have my reasons," he slowly said. "Do you work for the bank?"

"No, we work against the bank."

Solaire's eyes narrowed. "I don't understand."

She looked around and then leaned closer. "Before I say any more, I need to know who you work for."

"The people I work for want certain individuals at the bank held accountable for the financial meltdown."

"Are you referring to the bank's board members?"

Solaire nodded.

"Lady Marge Thatchburn?"

Solaire nodded.

"Sir Anthony Blairwood?"

Solaire nodded again.

"Lord Cornell Blacksmith?"

Solaire nodded once more.

She hesitated, but then she said, "Mr. Robbie Fisk?"

Solaire shook his head.

"Why not him?" she said.

"We don't believe he was responsible, but he may hold information that may be vital."

"I don't know if you are aware, but they found his car in the Thames."

"I am aware."

"He has not been seen in London."

"I know."

"He may be dead."

"Perhaps, but even dead people leave clues behind. I intend to find those clues and use them against RBL's board members."

She looked at him hard and then nodded. She looked over at Humphries, who came over.

"I'll have that drink now," she said.

Humphries looked at Solaire. "The same thing for you?"

"This time, no ice," he replied.

"Ice?" Emma raised an eyebrow.

"Iced tea, but no ice," Solaire said.

She smiled. "I'll try one too."

"Coming right up."

When Humphries was gone, Solaire said, "You said *we* work against the bank. Who were you referring to?"

She leaned closer. "SCABB."

"SCABB?" Solaire asked.

"The Secret Coalition Against Big Business. I know it doesn't sound glamorous, but it's not supposed to be."

Their drinks came.

She took a sip. "I haven't had iced tea since I was a kid."

"I'm still a kid," Solaire replied.

"Our goal is to push the government into not allowing businesses to get too big."

"You mean by acquisition, takeovers, or mergers?"

"Exactly. What's happening is big corporations are gobbling up small businesses, which leads to less competition, and hence the potential for monopolies or oligopolies. In some cases, the corporations become so large that they are deemed 'too big to fail.'"

"Like in the United States?"

"Yes. RBL was allowed to become too big for its own good. No one in parliament said anything, and do you know why?"

Solaire waited.

"They themselves had money invested in it. When the collapse happened, the first thing parliament did was bail them out, therefore allowing them to recoup their losses via taxpayers' money. But this wasn't the end of it. The regular citizens who had invested in RBL lost everything. Parliament did nothing to bail them out because *they* were considered to have made bad investment decisions. Talk about hypocrisy!"

Solaire took the information in. "Why the word 'secret' in SCABB?"

"Right now, we prefer to stay under the radar, but we are involved in rallies, protests, and demonstrations throughout London. There are a lot of powerful individuals and companies who want us shut down. Our hope is that one day SCABB will no longer be needed, but until then, we will fight for what is right."

"What is it that you want from me?" Solaire asked.

"If what you are saying is true, then we want to help you."

"How?"

"In whatever capacity you require."

Solaire finished his drink and got up.

"How can I contact you?" he asked.

She wrote her number on a napkin.

Solaire took it and put it in his pocket.

"It was a pleasure meeting you," he said.

"Same here," she said with a smile.

***

The next morning, Solaire went down to the nearest café and had a hearty breakfast, which consisted of two omelets, potatoes, toast, and a cup of tea.

He returned to his flat and spent the next hour researching Louise Mapother, RBL's extra affairs liaison.

Mapother had been with RBL for over twenty years. She controlled every aspect of RBL's public image. No interviews were allowed with the media without her permission. No meetings took place without her knowledge. And no individuals were invited to RBL's functions without her scrutiny.

If Solaire wanted to get into RBL's party, then he needed a good cover story.

He spent the remainder of the morning working on his laptop.

First, he updated a fictitious website he had used in his prior assignments, and then he prepared business cards that matched the website.

When he was done, Roman Solaire of Travers Private Equity Firm was born.

Mr. Solaire was someone who could invest generously in RBL's various portfolios.

***

Solaire looked at his watch.

It was almost lunch time.

He stood across the street from RBL's headquarters.

He adjusted his baseball cap and pulled his jacket collar up.

As if on cue, David Clampton emerged from the building and began walking away from it.

Solaire knew exactly where he was going: to his favorite restaurant.

Solaire quickly crossed the road, brushed past Clampton, and then headed for RBL's headquarters.

In his hand was Clampton's access card.

As Solaire approached the front doors, he was relieved the doorman who had taken his hundred-pound note a day earlier was not on duty.

The doorman held the door open, and Solaire entered.

RBL's front lobby was far grander than anything Solaire had ever seen. The ceiling reached three stories high. Huge columns stood on either side of him. The recently polished marble floor glistened.

Everything about it said *expensive.*

A guard stood to the side.

There were many people coming in and out, so the guard didn't pay any particular attention to Solaire.

Solaire walked up to the building's directory, which was placed on the wall, and examined it.

Louise Mapother's office was on the seventh floor.

He then searched for Robbie Fisk. His office was on the highest floor: eleventh.

Solaire took the elevator to the seventh floor.

There was a long hall with paintings hanging on both sides.

Solaire moved down the hall until, behind a glass wall, he spotted Mapother's office.

Her secretary was behind a desk typing away on a computer.

Solaire retreated to the elevator.

He took it to the sixth floor.

When he got off, he quickly searched for the fire alarm switch.

He looked at his watch and then pulled the alarm.

Instantly a bell went off.

Solaire rushed up the stairs and was back on the seventh floor.

Through the glass wall, he could see Mapother's assistant had a bewildered look on her face.

Solaire headed for the bathroom and hid in one of the stalls.

He looked at his watch again.

When two minutes had gone by, he emerged from the bathroom and headed for Mapother's office.

He scanned Clampton's card and entered.

The office was empty.

Solaire rushed to the secretary's desk.

As he expected, the computer was locked.

Solaire pulled out a USB key and put it into the slot.

He then restarted the computer.

When it came back on, the software on the USB began to load.

It gave Solaire a temporary password, which he memorized.

He removed the USB, restarted the computer, and entered the temporary password.

This all took less than three minutes.

Solaire found the secretary's calendar.

He entered a memo indicating that Ms. Mapother should call Mr. Roman Solaire back regarding an invitation to their upcoming party.

Solaire restarted the computer and left.

He looked at his watch again. By now, the security team would have gone through every inch of the sixth floor.

Solaire didn't have much time.

He took the stairs up to the eleventh floor.

The floor was vacant.

He quickly searched and found Fisk's office.

Solaire scanned the card and ducked underneath the police tape.

Fisk's office was spacious. It had large floor-to-ceiling windows. On the left was a stylish, modern desk with a leather chair. In the middle were white leather chairs and a cappuccino-colored coffee table with business magazines on it.

There was something odd about the way they were placed.

Instead of being spread over the table, they were neatly stacked on top of one another.

On the left side of the office were large wooden shelves.

Solaire walked over to them.

Books lined the top shelves.

In the middle were various awards and other random items.

Solaire picked up one of the awards. It was for Businessman of the Year.

Solaire spotted a tray with bottles and glasses.

Solaire examined one of the bottles, lifted the cap, and sniffed.

Whiskey.

He examined one of the glasses.

They were clean—too clean for someone who hadn't been in his office for quite some time.

Everything about the office looked too orderly as if it had been thoroughly searched.

Whatever Solaire was hoping to find was either not here or had already been found.

Solaire walked over to Fisk's desk.

Like everything else, his desk looked spotless and organized. Solaire was certain it had been combed through, and so had the computer.

There was a framed photo on Fisk's desk.

Solaire picked it up. It was of Robbie Fisk and his wife.

Suddenly there was a noise from the elevator bank.

The elevators were running again.

Solaire instantly moved to the corner, where it was darkest.

RBL's employees were returning to their desks.

He was sure he had more time, but they may have realized sooner that it was a false alarm.

Solaire hid in the shadows and watched.

More people emerged from the elevators.

Soon the floor would be crawling with people.

He waited for the right moment before he quickly rushed over, slid the glass doors open, and left Fisk's office.

As he was walking toward the stairs, a hand grabbed his shoulder.

Solaire turned.

A large man wearing a suit said, "Hey, the elevators are working now. You can use them."

"Um, yes," Solaire said. "Thank you. I will."

"No problem," the man said, smiling.

Solaire took the elevator down.

He quickly raced out of RBL's headquarters.

Outside he spotted David Clampton.

Someone must have informed him about the alarm at RBL. Clampton didn't look happy about being pulled out of his lunch.

Solaire finally allowed himself to smile.

His initial plan when he had first seen Clampton was to procure his access card and search Fisk's office. Now he was able to not only go through Fisk's office but also invite himself to RBL's exclusive party.

***

Solaire sat back on a comfortable leather chair and surveyed the surroundings.

The Penthouse Suite at the Sheraton Park Tower was a stylish one-bedroom suite with a historic view of Knightsbridge. It came with the basic amenities: a plasma TV in the bedroom and lounge, a walk-in wardrobe, a lavish bathroom detailed in marble with plush bathrobes and slippers, and an opulent bedroom with cotton sheets and plump pillows piled high.

It was luxurious, to say the least.

*For £3,500 a night, it better be*, Solaire thought.

The only reason he had selected the Knightsbridge Suite was that rumor had it that Muhammad Ali had stayed in it.

How true this was, Solaire didn't know or care.

He wanted to experience what the "Greatest" may have experienced.

There was a knock at the door.

"Talk about expensive," Levack said as Solaire opened the door.

"Come in," Solaire said.

Levack whistled as he took in the room. "They don't spare any expenses, do they?"

"Can I order you anything?" Solaire asked.

Levack plopped himself on a chair and felt the leather exterior. "Yeah, why not? I'll have a…" He stopped and then smiled. "I would love a spot of tea," he said in his fake British accent. "With crumpets."

"Right," Solaire said, and he ordered.

"Nice," Levack said, admiring the room. "They give you a nice budget, huh?"

"Yes, I suppose," Solaire said as he sat down across from him.

"Pricey?" Levack inquired.

"Very."

Levack nodded. "I wish they gave me a nice budget."

"Where are you staying?" Solaire asked.

Levack gave him a devilish smile. "It's for me to know and for you *not* to find out."

Solaire was becoming accustomed to Levack's secrecy.

"Where I'm staying, it's nothing spectacular, I promise you," Levack added. "I'm a company man on company dime, as they say."

Solaire didn't say anything.

"What can I do for you?" Levack asked.

There was a knock at the door.

A butler entered with a tray and placed it on the table before them.

"Is there anything else, sir?" he politely asked.

"It's fine, thank you," Solaire replied.

The butler bowed and left.

"Oh, goodie." Levack rubbed his hands. "Would you like some?" he asked, still using his British accent.

"I'm good."

Levack poured the hot liquid in a cup, added some milk, dropped in two lumps of sugar, gently stirred, and tapped the side of the cup with the spoon. Then he lifted the cup with his pinky raised to the sky, and he sipped.

"Marvelous," he finally said.

Solaire wanted to roll his eyes, but the telephone rang.

He lifted the receiver. "Yes, put her through." He listened, spoke a few words, and then hung up.

"Who was it?" Levack asked, taking a bite of crumpet.

"I've just been invited to the Royal Bank of Lords' annual party."

Levack raised an eyebrow.

"I need you to do scouting of the location. I need to know the entire layout of it. Important people will be attending. These people are linked to RBL. I am certain that vital information will be passed among them. If I know where they will be congregating, then I can make myself available there."

"And where is this event being held?"

"I don't know yet. The private invitation should be arriving soon."

"Ah, I see." Levack nodded. "Is this why you are here in this fancy hotel—for appearances?"

Solaire smiled. "Roman Solaire of Travers Private Equity Firm only travels first class."

***

The taxi driver dropped Solaire off in front of a Pakistani restaurant in Southall, a suburban district in west London.

Earlier, he had called Emma Morgan and asked her to meet him.

She had given him this restaurant's address.

A waiter escorted him to a table near the windows.

Solaire ordered a glass of water and waited.

The restaurant was starting to get busy. Solaire glanced out the window and saw the sun coming down.

Fifteen minutes later, a car drove up to the restaurant, and out came Emma Morgan.

She entered the restaurant and was escorted to his table.

She was wearing a blue dress that was mid-length. Her blonde hair was pulled back in a ponytail.

"Sorry to keep you waiting," she said, taking a seat.

"It's all right," Solaire said. "I was early."

The waiter came over. Emma ordered a glass of wine.

When Solaire declined, she asked, "You don't drink, Mr. Solaire?"

"Nothing hard, I'm afraid. My stomach is quite sensitive. And it's Roman."

She blushed. "I'm sure in your line of work, you need a strong stomach."

Solaire raised an eyebrow. "My line of work?"

"I mean, going after high-level bankers."

Solaire smiled.

"I was wondering, Ms. Morgan—" Solaire said.

"Call me Emma."

"Emma, the person who drove you here… is he your boyfriend?"

"You mean Sean?" She laughed. "Sean's my brother and the president of SCABB."

"Then, I would have loved to meet him."

"You will," she said. "I told him about you, but he's still a little cautious."

"He's not sure if he can trust me?" Solaire said.

"I hope to alleviate that tonight."

Solaire grinned. "Ah, I see."

"What?"

"Here I thought I was going to find out some information about you, but instead you are here to find out something about me."

"I think that's fair. We both get what we want."

"Indeed."

The waiter returned.

Emma ordered karahi chicken while he ordered butter chicken.

"What would you like to know about me?" Solaire asked.

"Who are you?" Emma replied.

"Who am I? I am Roman Solaire," Solaire said with his arms wide out.

She laughed. "I can't say I have heard of you."

"Which is precisely how I want it."

"Where were you born?"

"Montreal, but I was raised in Toronto."

"A person from the Commonwealth?" she said in a regal accent.

"Solaire bowed. "Yes, your majesty."

"And what do you do?"

"As my employer likes to say, I find that one thing which otherwise cannot be found."

"Sounds complicated and dangerous."

"It is.'"

Their meals came.

Along with the chicken, there was rice, naan, and chutney on the side.

"Who do you work for?" she asked between bites.

"I'm afraid I can't say, but I assure you we're the good guys."

"That's good to know," she said half-heartedly.

Solaire pulled out a card and placed it in front of her. "For now, you can assume I work there."

"Travers Private Equity Firm?"

Solaire nodded. "And as the head of the firm, I have been invited to RBL's annual party."

"I heard it's very exclusive."

"It is, and I would like to bring you as my date."

She stopped eating.

"This will get *you* closer to RBL's board members, and *I* will have a beautiful lady by my side."

She blushed.

"But first, I would like to know a little about you," Solaire said. "To make sure you are right for the position. There are other candidates, you know."

"Are there?" she asked teasingly.

"Yes, ma'am. All candidates will go through a rigorous selection process."

"Will they?" She leaned forward. "Do all of them go to a fancy restaurant?"

Solaire shook his head. "Only a select few."

She laughed. "Okay, I was born and raised in Brighton. I went to the University of Sussex, graduating in Cultural and Community Studies. After that, I worked for various organizations, and now I devote my time fully to SCABB."

"Interesting," Solaire said. "What about your family?"

"Well, my mom and dad got married when they were still teenagers, and so it didn't last. My dad went off to Oxford, and my mom stayed behind and raised me. I didn't know who my father was for a very long time. I was raised by my stepfather."

"Sean's your stepbrother?"

"Yeah, but he might as well be my, quote-unquote, real brother. We are inseparable."

"What about your biological father? Where is he?"

She paused and looked away.

"I'm sorry," Solaire said. "That was insensitive of me. It's none of my business."

"No, it's okay. I found out recently when my mom got sick. I confronted him. At first, he didn't believe I was his daughter, but now he has done everything in his power to help me." She paused and then said, "You have to realize that both my parents were very young when they got married, and both had different plans for their lives. My dad became focused on his education, and my mom focused on me."

Their desserts came. Rasmalai—milk dumplings served in thickened milk.

"Sweet," Solaire said, sipping the milk.

"You haven't had it before?" Emma asked.

Solaire shook his head.

"My favorite," she said. "I love Indian food."

"I find it's either too spicy or too sweet," he said.

"What do you have planned for the members of RBL?" she asked.

"Find evidence against them and prosecute them."

She looked at him. "Who'll prosecute them? I don't know if you know, but they are strongly linked to British high society."

"I know, but we won't prosecute them in Britain."

Emma looked confused. "Then where?"

"Somewhere else."

He gave her a wide smile.

"There's something you are not telling me," she said.

"Right now, I would rather keep my cards close to me—for your own safety, of course."

"Of course," she said.

Solaire paused for a moment. He snapped his fingers. "Damn. I forgot one thing. RBL does not know about you somehow, do they?"

Emma laughed. "My group is secret, remember?"

Solaire smiled. "Yes, that's right."

As they finished their desserts, Solaire said to Emma, "Why don't you show me around London? I am only here for a short time."

"I would love to, but Sean and I have work to do tonight."

Solaire smiled. "Some other time then."

***

Solaire spent the next morning scouring Savile Row. It was famous for its bespoke men's tailoring and had a history going back two hundred and fifty years. Its customers had included dignitaries, presidents, heads of state, and kings and maharajahs.

The tailored suits could cost thousands of pounds but required weeks to be made. Solaire searched with little hope that he could get one sooner—much sooner. Fortunately, one shop had a tailored suit, which a client had failed to pick up for quite some time. With minor alterations, the suit fit Solaire like a glove.

His next stop was for a luxury car rental.

At five hundred pounds a day, Solaire selected one of the finest cars they had available.

He then went to a café, where he met Donald Levack.

Levack had a somber look on his face. "The place is surrounded by ten-foot-high walls. The only way in is through the front gates, which has security guards. I also noticed as I passed by that it had several CCTV cameras around the perimeter." Levack pulled out a folder. "But that didn't mean I didn't find anything. I spoke to a real estate agent, and apparently, Upper Town Court is a private mansion, one of the most luxurious estates in all of England. It has over a hundred rooms, many of which are bedrooms. It has several swimming pools, a squash court, tennis court, wine cellar, and even a panic room."

"A panic room?" Solaire asked, surprised.

"Yes, it's for when—"

"I know what it's for. Please continue."

"Yeah, well, it's surrounded by over fifty acres of land. It has a garage which can hold a dozen luxury cars, a private cinema, and oh, it also has some of the finest marble from all over the world. That's what the real estate agent kept repeating." Levack looked up from the folder. "And get this, it's up for sale."

"What's the asking price?" Solaire inquired.

Levack raised an eyebrow. "Why? You're interested in buying it?"

Solaire shook his head. "Not quite, but that information may come in handy during my visit there."

"Well, let's say when converted to US dollars, it's over a hundred million."

"Expensive."

"You better believe it. And the current owners are in financial trouble because no one is willing to pay the asking price, so they have agreed to rent it out until they find a buyer."

"And RBL has rented it in order to host their party."

"Precisely, old chap," Levack said, smiling. "But I'd be careful if I were you."

Solaire waited.

"The security personnel don't belong to the estate. RBL has hired their own."

"Why would they do that?" Solaire said, more to himself than Levack.

"I guess they are expecting trouble."

***

Solaire pulled up in his gray Maserati Gran Turismo.

Emma Morgan was waiting for him on the steps of her building.

She wore a stunning green dress that went down to her ankles. Her hair was pulled back in a bun. She wore diamond earrings and a pearl necklace.

Solaire got out. He was wearing a charcoal gray suit with a white shirt and charcoal gray tie.

"Wow," she said.

"I can say the same thing," he said.

She smiled. "I meant the car."

"Well, I meant *you*."

She blushed.

He held the car door for her.

"Is this yours?" she asked.

"It is for tonight, at least."

***

The queue to get into the party was long.

Solaire counted almost twenty vehicles ahead of him.

The backup was due to security screening each vehicle before it entered the gates.

Solaire didn't feel out of place. He saw Bentleys, BMWs, Mercedes, Porsches, and even a couple of Rolls Royces.

"Are you certain we'll get in?" Emma asked.

"We'll find out."

They approached the gates, and a big, burly security guard came over.

He was holding a computerized tablet.

"Your name, sir?" he asked.

"Roman Solaire."

The guard typed it in.

"Do you have identification?" he asked.

Solaire supplied one.

"And your guest's, please."

Emma handed hers over.

Another guard came over.

"We'll need to do a routine checkup if you don't mind," the first guard said.

The second guard quickly scanned the interior of the vehicle.

"Can you please pop open the boot?" the first guard asked.

Solaire understood that he meant the trunk.

When the second guard was done, the first guard finally smiled and said, "Enjoy your evening, sir."

The drive to the mansion was long but beautiful. Tall, lush trees were on either side of them. They passed by gardens and ponds and a few birds and animals.

A valet rushed over when they reached the entrance.

Solaire and Emma got out, and Solaire handed the valet the keys.

"Take good care of it," he said.

He meant it. The car was, after all, a rental.

Solaire held his arm out, and Emma took it.

Together they entered Upper Town Court.

The grand foyer was indeed made of some of the finest marble in the world.

A man in a butler's uniform approached them with a tray.

"Champagne?" he asked.

Solaire took a glass with no intention of drinking it.

Emma took one too.

"I can't believe this," Emma said. "The average person is struggling to keep their homes while RBL is throwing money to rent a place like this."

"I suppose appearances are still important even in an economy such as this," Solaire said. *Not to mention the money I'm splurging to make* mine *look good*, he thought wryly.

They were escorted to the grounds area of the estate.

An orchestra was playing music on one side. Tables and chairs were placed on the other. In the middle were long tables with hors d'ouevres.

Solaire estimated that there were over a couple of hundred people present.

A woman came over. Solaire immediately recognized her.

"I'm Louise Mapother," she said.

"Thank you for the invitation, Ms. Mapother," Solaire said, shaking her hand.

"Your CV on your website was very impressive," she said. "It would have been a travesty not to have invited you."

"Thank you." Solaire introduced Emma.

"How do you do?" Emma said, smiling.

"Pleasure to meet you." Mapother smiled back. "Come, I would like you to meet some people."

Emma turned to Solaire. "I think I'll go sample the appetizers if you don't mind."

"Not at all."

Solaire followed Mapother through the party. They occasionally stopped to allow Mapother to greet some guests.

Finally, they reached the board members. The three of them were standing together as if in a huddle.

Blairwood, Thatchburn, and Blacksmith turned when Solaire and Mapother approached them.

Mapother introduced Solaire.

When the pleasantries were over, Blairwood said, "How long have you been in London, Mr. Solaire?"

"Only a few days," he replied.

"How long do you intend to stay?"

"Until all my work is done."

"You mean for your investment firm?" Thatchburn asked.

"Yes."

"Where are you situated?" Blacksmith interjected.

"Toronto."

"A Canadian firm?" Thatchburn said. "We don't get many investors from the Commonwealth."

"I assure you, we may be in Canada, but we have our hands everywhere," Solaire said.

Blairwood raised an eyebrow. "Indeed."

"Let me cut to the chase," Blacksmith said. "How much would you say your firm is willing to invest in London?"

"As much as needed," Solaire replied. "But only if the returns are stable and assured."

"I don't know about that," Blacksmith said. "In today's economy, nothing is guaranteed."

"But they are definitely not risky," Thatchburn said, giving Blacksmith a look.

"Ah, yes, we are heavily risk-averse," Blacksmith said. "We don't play with our investors' money. We treat it like it is our own."

"That is reassuring," Solaire said.

"Plus," Blairwood quickly said, "we are not like those American banks and their subprime rubbish."

"What do you invest in?" Solaire asked.

Blairwood leaned closer. "Gold, oil, natural gas—the necessities of life."

"Gold is a necessity?" Solaire asked.

"For the rich, it is," Thatchburn replied.

It was then that Solaire noticed the golden bracelet, golden rings, and golden earrings Thatchburn wore.

"When gold was less than five hundred dollars an ounce, I predicted it would go up," Thatchburn said proudly. "Now, it is *triple* that."

"We made a fortune on that speculation," Blairwood said.

"You mean your investors made a fortune," Solaire said.

"Yes, of course."

Solaire said, "It was sad to hear what happened to one of your board members, Mr. Robbie Fisk."

There was a pause before Thatchburn said, "Yes, we were all heartbroken."

"I read in the papers that he committed suicide?" Solaire said.

"Yes, well," Blacksmith said, "that's what Scotland Yard told us."

"Why would he do that?" Solaire asked.

Blairwood leaned closer. "If I can be frank with you, Mr. Solaire, Robbie was going through some personal issues."

"Women issues to be exact," Blacksmith quickly added.

"Scandalous," Thatchburn said, shaking her head.

"It may have been too much for him," Blairwood said.

"Do you suppose someone killed him?" Solaire asked.

There was dead silence.

"Why would anyone want to do that?" Thatchburn replied. "Robbie was one of us. He was family. I just can't imagine anything as horrific as that."

Other guests came over and greeted the three board members.

Blairwood leaned over to Solaire. "Maybe later we can sit and discuss how the Royal Bank of Lords can help with your investment needs."

"I would like that."

***

Solaire headed back to where he'd left Emma. On the way, something caught his eye.

A woman was standing in the distance. She had shoulder-length silver hair. She was wearing a silver business suit and matching silver shoes.

She was looking directly at him.

Solaire had the sudden urge to go up to her, but before he could, she turned and disappeared into the crowd.

Emma approached him.

"Did I miss anything important?" she asked.

"Not really," Solaire replied. "Only that the board is interested in doing business with me."

"Isn't that good?"

"Very."

A voice came over the speakers asking everyone to turn their attention to the south side of the estate.

A projector and screen had been set up there.

A video played, showing the history of the bank, followed by the transition the bank had undergone over the years, and finally ending with all the great work the bank had done for the local communities.

"They make it sound like RBL is a charitable organization," Emma whispered to Solaire.

All three board members came up to the microphone and thanked the guests for coming and for their loyalty to the bank in such difficult times. They briefly mentioned the loss of one of their board members.

Solaire noticed that Emma cringed whenever they mentioned Fisk's name.

"He's a good man," Emma said, biting her lip.

"Did you know him?" Solaire asked, turning to her.

Emma blinked and said, "No, I read about him. He seemed like he genuinely cared about those who had lost their life savings."

Solaire put his arm around her and looked directly in her eyes. "We are going to make sure that no one else loses their life savings."

She nodded.

The music came back up.

"Would you care to dance, Ms. Morgan?" Solaire asked with his arm extended.

"I would love to, Mr. Solaire," Emma replied, smiling.

***

They danced through a couple of songs before Solaire saw the three board members leave the party and head back into the estate.

"You will have to excuse me," he said to Emma. "I have to go to the men's room."

"I'll be right here," she said.

Solaire rushed past the other dancers and went up the stairs. With over a hundred rooms, he did not want to lose the board members.

He saw them going down a hall.

He followed but kept a fair distance.

They stopped by the elevator and took it up.

Solaire watched the numbers change, and when the elevator stopped on the third floor, he took the stairs from there.

He was halfway down the hall when a voice said, "Sir!"

He turned.

A man in a security uniform approached. "Sir, you're not allowed to be here."

"I am so sorry," Solaire said. "I was searching for the men's bathroom, and then I ended up here."

"There's one on the ground floor for the guests. I can escort you there."

"Is there one near here? I have to go *really* bad, I'm afraid."

Solaire made a face.

The guard looked at him and then said, "Right this way, sir."

They walked down the hall, stopping at a door.

"Once you're done, please return to the party," the guard said.

"I will make sure to do that. Thank you."

Solaire entered the bathroom and was taken aback by how exquisite it was. Everything from the counter to the bathtub was covered in intricately designed marble.

Solaire waited for the guard to get as far away as possible. He was about to leave the bathroom when suddenly the door swung open and a man entered.

The man's head was shaved. He wore a silver suit on his large body.

Solaire immediately went to the sinks. He turned on the taps.

The man moved past him and went to the other side of the sinks.

Solaire slowly washed up and then grabbed a hand towel.

As he was drying his hands, in the mirror, Solaire saw the man remove a knife from his jacket.

The man hid the knife behind his back.

He moved toward Solaire.

Solaire carefully twisted the towel in his hands.

Just as the man was about to swing the knife, Solaire turned. Using the hand towel as a weapon, he snapped it across the man's hand.

The man howled as the knife flew out of his hand and landed near the tub.

Solaire kicked the man in the gut, causing him to fall back.

Solaire raced toward the knife. The man quickly recovered and tackled him from behind.

He pushed Solaire to the wall.

Solaire's face hit the marble.

The man was strong, and his weight was crushing Solaire into the wall.

Solaire swung his elbow back, connecting across the man's jaw.

The man released his weight and stumbled back, holding his face.

Blood flowed into Solaire's left eye.

He tried to wipe it away, but in the mirror, he saw the man charge toward him with his head down.

Solaire instantly moved left. The man missed him by an inch and went straight into the mirror.

The man smashed his face, shattering glass.

He screamed as he stumbled back.

Solaire lowered himself into a crouch and tripped the man.

The man fell back, hitting his head on the side of the tub, then he rolled into it.

When Solaire checked, the man's head was twisted to one side. Blood covered the inside of the tub.

The man was dead.

Solaire fell to his knees.

He was drained.

He lowered his head and took a deep breath.

Blood dripped down his face.

Solaire lifted himself up and checked himself in one of the mirrors.

There was a deep cut above his left eyebrow.

Solaire turned on the taps, filled his hands with cold water, and splashed it on the cut.

It stung.

He grabbed one of the hand towels and placed it on the cut.

He applied pressure.

A few minutes later, it looked as if the blood had stopped flowing.

He then cleaned the wound with a wet towel.

He adjusted his shirt and tie, and he applied water to his hair.

When he felt he was ready, he went to the door.

He pulled it open and found himself facing the barrel of a gun.

The silver-haired woman was holding it.

"We've been waiting for you, Mr. Solaire," she said.

***

Solaire was taken to a room.

His arms and legs were tied to a chair.

The woman crossed her arms and looked directly at him.

"Do you expect me to tell you everything?" Solaire asked.

"That is so clichéd," the woman laughed. "You've been watching too many spy movies. And yes, I do expect that you'll tell me your entire life story. We are in the farthest corner of the estate— away from *everyone*. No one will come to your aid, and no one will hear your screams, Mr. Solaire."

"Are you planning on torturing me?" Solaire asked.

"It depends on your answers."

"I have a question for you."

"Okay." She smiled.

"Why were you trying to kill me?" Solaire asked. "The man in the bathroom is one of yours, is he not?"

"Yes, and if you hadn't put up a fight, it all might have ended painlessly for you." She walked around him. "You see, he was very skilled with a knife. One slice to the throat, and it would have been over very quickly. Who do you work for?"

"You did not answer *my* question."

Suddenly the door swung open, and in came David Clampton.

"He will tell you why," the woman said.

Clampton looked at him with disgust. "The cameras caught you in the bank's headquarters. You accessed areas and equipment that were strictly off-limits. *You* stole my access card. Do you have any idea how much trouble that got me in?"

"Who do you work for?" the woman asked, ignoring Clampton.

"You would not believe me even if I told you."

"Try me."

"An international organization that prosecutes criminals, and we have our eyes on the board members of the Royal Bank of Lords."

"Really?" the woman said, raising an eyebrow. "I didn't think white-collar crime would result in such drastic measures, and by that, I mean stealing security passes, breaking into corporate buildings, and falsely entering parties. It's just money."

"I suppose to you it is, but to those who lost everything, it is more than that. Their entire lives were destroyed by the recklessness of RBL's board members."

"I'm not here to discuss morality," she said. "What is the name of the organization you work for?"

"That, I'm afraid, is top secret."

"I hope it's worth risking your life for." She turned to a man standing in the back.

The man wore a silver suit like the one worn by the dead man in the bathroom.

"You dress them up in matching outfits," Solaire said. "How adorable."

"I'm glad you are enjoying yourself, Mr. Solaire. But you won't be for long."

The man came up to Solaire. He cracked his knuckles and then swung his fist into Solaire's midsection.

Solaire gasped.

He coughed hard.

"That's just the beginning," the woman said.

Solaire sucked air through his nostrils.

*Yes, I bet it is*, he thought.

"Okay, okay, I will tell you what you want to know," he said.

She smiled. "Why is it that I don't believe you?"

"Ask me a question." Solaire coughed some more.

She stared at him.

"All right. Who do you work for?" she asked.

"Travers Private Equity Firm."

She shook her head and nodded to the man again.

The man smiled and cracked his knuckles once more.

***

The door swung open again, and this time the three board members came in.

"You shouldn't be here," the woman said to them.

"Have you found out what he knows?" Blacksmith asked.

"I'm working on it."

Blairwood turned to Solaire. "Why are you asking questions about Robbie Fisk?"

"I should ask you the same question."

Blairwood stared at him.

"Mrs. Fisk mentioned a certain person matching your friend's description," Solaire nodded toward the woman, "who paid her a visit."

"Fisk is dead," Thatchburn said.

"And if I am guessing correctly, you had him killed," Solaire said.

Thatchburn shook her head. "No, but it's not that we didn't want to. Before we could take any action, he did it for us by driving his car into the Thames."

Solaire said, "Then the question I need to ask is… why did you want him dead?"

There was no response.

"Is it because he had incriminating evidence against you?" Solaire asked. "Something he was willing to provide to the authorities?"

Blacksmith replied, "It was only after his death that we realized he had something against us. I will admit that our assessment of Fisk was wrong. Until a couple of months ago, he was completely loyal to us and the bank. Fisk was as guilty as any of us for the financial crisis. Then suddenly, he had a change of heart. He wanted the bank to compensate for any and all losses incurred by the investors."

"And he was right to request that," Solaire said. "You had insurance against such losses. Either way, the bank would have come out of it in good standing. You chose not to do it."

"You have no idea how disastrous that would have been," Blairwood said.

"Not to mention, set a precedent," Thatchburn added.

"Can you imagine a bank repaying someone for bad investment advice?" Blairwood said.

"Isn't that what the government did when they bailed RBL out?" Solaire asked.

"Decisions were made," Blacksmith replied. "No one could have predicted how bad things would turn out. Banks all across Europe have taken a hit, and we were no exception. We did what we had to for the survival of the bank."

"You did what was best for *you*," Solaire said. "All three of your net worth has gone up since the financial meltdown. While everyone else lost everything, you gained much more than before. How do you explain that?"

There was silence.

"We don't owe you any explanations," Blacksmith said.

"Our shareholders are quite happy," Thatchburn said. "And we only answer to them."

They turned to leave.

"What are you going to do with him?" Blairwood asked the woman.

"What we should have done with Fisk," the woman replied.

***

The punches were hard and fast.

Solaire coughed up blood. His midsection was bruised and raw.

He was certain he had a broken a rib or two.

He tried to breathe, but it hurt when he did.

The man cracked his knuckles again.

He hit Solaire again and again.

"I can't watch this," Clampton said. "I'll see you when you're done."

He left.

The woman turned to Solaire. "I told you it would be painful."

Solaire tried to speak, but no words came out.

"Save your breath. You're going to need it." She turned to his abuser. "Finish him."

From his jacket pocket, the man pulled out a clear plastic bag.

He went around Solaire.

He placed the bag over Solaire's head and wrapped it tightly around his neck, constricting the airflow.

Solaire gasped.

He tried thrashing his body this way and that, but the man held the bag firmly in place.

The bag inflated and deflated as Solaire tried to breathe, but it was futile. He was suffocating.

He felt dizzy and lightheaded.

Suddenly someone burst through the door.

"What is it?" the woman demanded.

"We have a problem outside. You need to come right away."

Solaire's abuser released his grip.

Air flowed into the bag.

Solaire inhaled deeply, and it felt good.

The woman turned to his abuser. "Do it quick and get rid of the body."

The woman, along with her other men, left.

Solaire was now alone with his abuser.

The man cracked his knuckles, and a smile spread over his face.

The man swung his fist at Solaire's midsection.

*Watch this*, Solaire thought.

He leaned forward and twisted.

The man's fist hit the side of the chair.

He winced, staggering back, holding his hand.

Solaire was barely upright. With his arms and legs tied to the chair, he placed all his weight on his toes.

Before the man could recover, Solaire threw his body onto him.

The back of the chair hit the man squarely across the head.

The man fell back with Solaire on top of him.

The impact snapped the arm of the chair in two. Pain shot through Solaire's arm. He quickly slid the ropes off the broken piece and then freed himself.

The man shook his head and tried to get back on his feet.

Solaire grabbed the broken piece and swung it across the man's face.

The man's head jerked back, and he fell to the ground hard.

Blood poured out through his nose.

The man's eyes rolled up.

He was dead.

Solaire felt no remorse. He pulled off the plastic bag and dropped to the ground, exhausted.

He knew he couldn't stay here.

They would come back, and if they found him, they would find a quicker way to kill him.

He thought about going through the door but was uncertain as to how many guards were outside.

He opened the window and looked down.

There was a balcony on the floor below him.

He pulled off his suit jacket and loosened his tie.

He carefully pulled himself up onto the windowsill and then over it.

Outside, he firmly clung to the edges of the window.

He estimated how far he was from the balcony below and then let go.

He landed on concrete.

Pain shot through him.

He didn't have time to worry about the damage to his body. He jumped over the balcony.

This time he landed on dirt and grass.

He got on his feet and rushed away from the estate as fast as he could.

His entire body was on fire.

He moved past trees and bushes.

He remembered Levack telling him the estate was surrounded by fifty acres of land.

Solaire didn't know how long he had run, but he saw a fence before him. Beyond the fence was a road.

*I hope that fence isn't live*, he thought. *The last thing I want is to be zapped after twice escaping death.*

He grabbed a branch and threw it at the fence.

The branch hit metal and then fell to the ground.

Solaire estimated the fence was eight feet high.

He pulled himself up and over it.

On the road, he began walking away from Upper Town Court.

He was not even a mile away when a car appeared.

Solaire felt a surge of hope.

The car stopped, and out came Emma Morgan.

"Oh my god," she cried, looking at him.

She helped him get into the back seat.

Solaire immediately recognized the driver. It was Sean, Emma's stepbrother.

He put his head back on the seat.

A million questions were swirling in his head, but before he could ask even one, he passed out.

***

Solaire opened his eyes to darkness.

He blinked and then blinked some more.

He tried to get up, but his entire body felt rooted to where he lay.

He scanned his surroundings and quickly realized he was in a room.

He heard sounds.

He listened.

They were voices, and they were coming from another room.

He slowly lifted his head and then willed his body up.

Every inch of him was in pain.

He touched a bandage above his left eye. It was bulky.

He moved his hands over his midsection. It was wrapped in white cloth. He tried to inhale deeply but stopped when it became unbearable. He took short breaths. It hurt less.

His knuckles were sore and bruised.

He left the room and was in another room—this one bigger.

There was a television and a sofa on one side, a kitchen on the other, and a table with chairs in the middle.

Emma and Sean were at the table, going over some papers.

They stopped when they saw him.

"You shouldn't be up," Emma said, coming over.

She looked him over to make sure all the bandages and wraps were still in place.

"Where am I?" he asked.

"My apartment," Sean said. "By the way, I'm—"

"Sean," Solaire said. "Emma told me."

Sean said, "Can I get you anything? Tea, perhaps."

"Tea is fine. But make it strong."

"Right away," Sean said, going into the kitchen.

"How are you feeling?" Emma asked.

"Like someone who just went through a meat grinder."

Emma smirked. "Well, at least you came out in one piece."

He slowly made his way to the sofa and sat down.

He rubbed his eyes. "What happened last night?"

Sean came over and placed the steaming cup before him. "We rescued you," he replied.

Solaire waited for more.

Emma said, "When you didn't return from the estate, I knew something was wrong. I called Sean. He provided the diversion."

"Diversion?" Solaire was confused.

Sean replied, "When Emma called and told me, I quickly assembled a large protest outside the party."

"How were you able to do it that fast?" Solaire asked.

Sean smiled. "Technology is every protestor's dream. I posted a message on our website, which instantly passed it on to each and every one of our members, and voila! Two hundred loud and angry demonstrators were outside the gates of Upper Town Court."

Emma said, "When I saw most of the security guards go toward the front gates, I went inside searching for you. But it was like searching for someone at a carnival. The estate had too many rooms to go through. I doubled back and caught up with Sean. We hoped you had gotten away, but we weren't certain until we saw you by the road."

"Thank you," Solaire finally said. He took a sip of tea.

"Emma told me what you are doing," Sean said. "SCABB is here to help in any way."

"What did you find out?" Emma asked him.

Solaire shook his head. "Nothing of importance."

"It was all for nothing," Emma said, looking sad.

"Not exactly," Solaire said. "We now know we are dealing with dangerous people—people who are capable of anything, even murder."

"What are you going to do?" she asked.

"First, I am going to need some strong painkillers. Then I'm going to go after them."

***

Solaire watched through dark sunglasses as tourists strolled by him.

They were easy to spot. They were either holding some sort of guidebook or camera.

If that didn't give them away, it was the way they looked at everything in awe and wonder.

London had some of the most recognizable sights in the world—the London Bridge, the House of Parliament, and Big Ben.

Right now, he was staring up at London's most recent attraction, the London Eye.

He watched a man buy a ticket.

Solaire had already bought his.

He followed the man to a giant capsule, which was on a Ferris wheel. The wheel moved slowly, allowing passengers inside the capsule to get a panoramic view of London.

The man sat on a wooden bench in the middle. The other passengers circled the giant windows, taking pictures and videos.

Solaire sat beside the man.

"You look terrible," Travers said.

"I feel even worse."

"I could—"

"No," Solaire cut him off. He knew what Travers was about to say, and he wanted nothing to do with it. Solaire hated guns, ever since he was a child. Regardless of what gun-nuts proclaimed, that it's not guns killing people but people killing people, Solaire knew guns made it easier.

"Then utilize Levack," Travers said. "He is becoming restless."

Solaire nodded.

"After speaking to you, I made some calls," Travers said. "The woman in silver? Her name is Claudia Cain. She is a freelancer, working for the highest bidder. In this case, it is RBL."

"What have they hired her for?" Solaire asked.

"It seems what we have hired you for."

Solaire looked at him.

"Cain is searching for incriminating evidence Fisk may have left behind."

"How does she know there is even any evidence to begin with?"

Travers went silent.

"There is something you are not telling me," Solaire said.

"The day before Fisk disappeared, he had made a phone call to an anonymous person—a woman. He made a mistake by using his office phone. He did not realize at the time that he was under surveillance. Apparently, for the past couple of months, his behavior had become strange, and fearing a public relations disaster, the other board members had made an effort to keep tabs on him. In their defense, they were worried that Fisk was having an affair, and they just didn't want the negative publicity. What they overheard instead was Fisk describing certain documents in his possession that might shake RBL to its foundation."

"What type of documents?" Solaire asked.

"We don't know."

"Who recorded it?"

"David Clampton."

Solaire nodded.

"Why didn't you tell me this at the beginning?" Solaire asked. "In fact, why did you not just give me the recording?"

Travers looked away. "It is not as simple as you may think."

Solaire leaned over and whispered, "I almost died. Simple is not the answer I am looking for."

Travers sighed. "The recording was acquired without legal means."

"It was stolen?"

"Yes."

"By whom?"

Travers said nothing.

"You?" Solaire finally asked.

Travers nodded.

"I don't understand why that is an issue."

"CIL cannot be linked to anything irregular. What I did broke the law. It would have been inadmissible in court anyway."

"But what I do isn't exactly by the law," Solaire said.

"But you are not linked to CIL."

Solaire understood. As far as anyone knew, Roman Solaire did not officially work for the Court of International Law. According to Travers, he was an advisor, while Levack was a hired consultant.

"I should have told you," Travers said. "I didn't know this woman Cain was also involved. I am sorry, Roman."

Solaire said nothing.

They were coming to the end of their journey.

Solaire got up. "Tell Levack to meet me at my flat in St. John's Wood. We've got a lot of work to do."

***

"What is the link between RBL's board members and Claudia Cain?" Solaire asked.

Levack was sitting on a sofa, sipping a drink while Solaire was standing, staring out the window.

Levack shrugged. "Is this a multiple-choice question?"

"David Clampton," Solaire answered, ignoring his comment. "Clampton is the head of security for RBL. He was the one who bugged Fisk's phone. He was also the one who hired Cain."

"Okay, but I don't see where you're going with this," Levack said, scratching his head. "I have to tell you. I didn't have my bowl of cereal this morning."

Solaire again ignored Levack. "Clampton is the key to all of this."

"How?" Levack asked.

"Just ask yourself: why did Fisk decide to end his life?"

"Maybe he was guilty as sin, and his conscience couldn't take it anymore, so he decided to jump in the river," Levack said. "Personally, a bullet to the head would have been simpler."

"But why on that particular day?" Solaire asked.

"I don't know." Levack put his hands up in defeat. "Maybe it was his birthday."

Solaire placed an old newspaper in front of him.

"It was on this day that RBL reported one of their biggest losses ever."

Levack picked up the newspaper and scanned it.

"So?" he finally said. "Maybe he didn't want to face the media after that huge loss."

"The investors lost money, yes, but RBL was insured against such losses. So, why would Fisk kill himself on the day *he* made a lot of money?" Seeing Levack's blank face, Solaire said, "Because he didn't kill himself—he was murdered."

Levack sat up straight, "But didn't you say the board members denied having anything to do with his death?"

"They claimed so only because they were too late to do anything, but Clampton knew. He had the recording the day *before* Fisk disappeared. He only made it available to the other board members after what happened to Fisk, and I'm assuming it was then that the board members asked him to find that evidence, which led him to hire Cain."

"What you're saying," Levack said, "is if we get Clampton, we solve this case."

"Precisely."

***

"Are you certain this was the best choice for a vehicle?" Solaire asked.

Both he and Levack were inside a MINI Cooper. The Cooper was red with a Union Jack decal on the roof.

"Why do you ask?" Levack said.

"I mean, we're in a stakeout. Wouldn't this give us away?"

"No." Levack shook his head. "We're in England. All Brits drive this car."

Solaire looked around, but he didn't see a single MINI anywhere.

Across from them was RBL's headquarters.

"You sure he's going to come out?" Levack asked.

Solaire looked at his watch. "Any minute now."

As if on cue, Clampton emerged from the building and began walking in the direction of his favorite restaurant for his afternoon meal.

Levack put the MINI in gear.

He drove slowly, matching Clampton's pace.

Up ahead was a side street.

Levack accelerated, turned, and cut into Clampton's path.

Before Clampton could react, both Solaire and Levack were out.

"Get in," Levack said. He pulled his jacket back, revealing his firearm.

Clampton nodded and quickly did as he was told.

With Clampton in the back seat, they drove away.

"I told you this car would be perfect," Levack said, driving. "With no back doors, he can't escape."

"I thought you were dead?" Clampton said.

Solaire turned to face him. "I'm not."

"What do you want from me?" Clampton asked.

"Why did you kill Fisk?" Solaire replied.

"I didn't."

"Why is it that I don't believe you," Solaire said.

"I swear."

"Then what happened?"

Clampton went silent.

Levack glanced into the rear-view mirror. "Do you want me to stop the car? Because if I do, I'll bring my friend out again, and I promise you that it'll be the last thing you see."

"Don't shoot me. I'll tell you everything." Clampton turned to Solaire. "I followed Fisk in my car through London, but then I lost him, and before I knew what happened, his car was in the Thames."

"Why were you following him?" Solaire asked.

Clampton's shoulders sank. "I was trying to get money out of him."

"You were blackmailing him?" Solaire asked.

"Yes."

Clampton sighed.

"Classy," Levack said.

"I saw how much money everyone was making…"

"You mean the board members?" Solaire asked.

"Yes. While they were making millions, I was barely making ends meet."

"Why Fisk?"

"He was not as careful as the others. They'd been under public scrutiny for years, so they were always cautious. There are things even I don't know about them, and I'm RBL's head of security."

"How were you going to blackmail Fisk?"

"There were rumors swirling around that Fisk was seeing another woman. His behavior changed around this time as well. The board members asked me to keep an eye on him. I knew that was my chance. I started recording his conversations, but he was careful. He made sure to never use his office phone. Until one day—"

"When you overhead him say he had information against RBL," Solaire finished for him.

Clampton's eyes widened. "You know about it?"

"We know a lot of things, pal," Levack interjected.

"Go on," Solaire said.

"After Fisk died, what could I do then? I couldn't blackmail him, could I? I showed the tapes to the board members, but soon after, I lost one of the tapes."

Solaire thought of Travers but said nothing.

"Why did you hire Claudia Cain?" Solaire asked.

"The board members were bloody well freaked out. If anyone found that evidence, they'd be ruined, so I hired her to appease them."

"But you had no intention of her finding that information?" Solaire asked.

Clampton lowered his eyes. "No."

"Why not?"

"I wanted to find it so I could use it against them."

"You wanted to blackmail the board members?"

"Yes."

The MINI moved through the London streets, occasionally going around the roundabouts.

"You know where the evidence is?" Solaire asked.

Clampton nodded. "But I'm not a hundred percent sure."

"Take us there."

****

Across the street was a self-storage facility. They were in the MINI, looking directly at it.

"You think it's in there?" Solaire asked.

Clampton shrugged. "Sure."

"How sure?"

Levack turned and stared at him.

"On the day I was trailing Fisk, he made a stop at this location. I figure he either took something or left something in there."

"So, you're not sure," Levack said, shaking his head.

"No, but we can't ask Fisk now, can we?" Clampton said.

"Don't get smart," Levack warned.

Clampton crossed his arms and said, "Good luck trying to find it, though. There are over a hundred units in there. Plus, there are security guards and security cameras everywhere, and you need a proximity card to get through the front gates. It's not as simple as you think. Believe me, I tried."

Solaire looked at the facility.

The gate was open during business hours, and a manager was inside during this time.

A blue van approached the building and then went in.

"Wait here," Solaire said and got out.

"Where're you going?" Levack asked.

"I'll be back," Solaire said.

Levack stared at the rear-view mirror. "You behave yourself, okay?" he said to Clampton. "Or else I *will* shoot you. I haven't used my gun once in London, and I am itching to."

Clampton lowered himself in the back seat.

Twenty-five minutes later, Solaire returned and got in the passenger seat.

"Let's go," he said.

"Where?" Levack asked.

"Anywhere, but we have to come back when the facility closes."

"We're going to break into it later?" Levack inquired.

"We don't need to." Solaire pulled out a card. "I was able to procure this from the family in the blue van. I then went to the manager and told her I had forgotten where my storage unit was because I had not used it in quite some time. She asked me for the name on the lease. I said I wasn't sure because I had purchased it off an auction some years back. I rattled off some names, the common ones first: Robbie Fisk, Stacey Fisk, and Fisk's kids' name, but none came up. I showed the manager that I did indeed have a pass, just not the location of my unit. Seeing how frustrated I was, she mentioned some names, and one of them was the one."

"Which one?" Clampton asked, sitting straight up.

"Wouldn't you like to know?" Levack shot back.

"Stacey Glenister—her name before marrying Robbie Fisk."

Levack smiled. "You, my friend, are worth every penny."

"Okay, now that you know where it is, can I go?" Clampton asked.

"Not a chance, pal," Levack replied. "We wouldn't want you calling your friends, would we?"

"I wouldn't. I promise."

"Why is it that we don't trust you?" Levack said.

Solaire said, "You help us find what we're looking for, and we'll let you go."

"Why is it *I* don't trust *you*?" Clampton said.

"I give you my word," Solaire said.

"Plus, you got no choice," Levack added.

Clampton reluctantly nodded.

Levack started the MINI, and they were off.

***

Two hours later, they were back in the same spot they were in earlier.

This time the facility's gates were closed.

The MINI pulled up to the gates. Solaire held the card up to a black panel and waited. There was a beep, and the gates slid open.

They parked and then went inside.

"It's on the top floor," Solaire said. He was carrying a small bag.

They took a freight elevator up.

They were confronted with several rows, and each one contained many storage units.

"You go ahead," Levack said. "I'm going to check something out first."

Solaire and Clampton moved up.

They entered a row and then stopped.

"It should be this one," Solaire said.

The unit was covered with a roll-up metal door. A U-lock was attached at the base.

From the bag, Solaire pulled out a lock cutter and snapped the lock off.

He pulled the metal door up.

The storage unit was twenty by twenty, windowless, and surrounded by corrugated metal. It was the size of a two-car garage.

Solaire switched on a light.

The unit was filled with all sorts of objects. There were boxes upon boxes in the back, painted frames lay to one side, shelves filled with odds and ends to another side, and folded tables and chairs lay in the middle. There were electronic items such as an old computer with monitors next to it. Even kitchen utensils were placed among the items.

"How are we going to find it?" Clampton asked.

"Check the boxes first. See if they are labeled."

Levack returned.

"Whoa," he said. "That's a lot of junk."

"Then help us go through it," Solaire said.

Three hours went by, and they failed to find anything.

"I guess it's not here," Levack said.

"It has to be," Clampton said. "Where else would he keep it?"

"I don't know," Solaire said, in deep thought.

"Can I go?" Clampton asked. "I helped you as you wanted. You gave me your word."

Solaire looked over at Levack and then nodded. "You can go."

"No one is going anywhere," a voice said.

They turned.

***

Claudia Cain stood at the door of the unit. Beside her were two men. Each man was holding a weapon.

"Thank goodness you're here," Clampton said. "These two had me as their hostage."

"Shut up," Cain said.

"How did you find us?" Solaire asked.

"His cell phone," she replied, nodding toward Clampton. "We put a tracker in it."

"How did you get in?" Solaire asked.

"The security guard was kind enough to let us in." She had a smile on her face that told Solaire the guard didn't make it.

"I'm so glad I hired you," Clampton said, smiling. "Now shoot these two."

Cain pulled out a silver gun from her pocket and aimed it at him.

"What? What are you doing?" Clampton asked, flabbergasted.

"I don't work for *you*," she replied. "I work for the board of RBL, and they no longer trust you."

Clampton turned pale.

"The board had started to get suspicious when you failed to report certain information on time."

"You mean the recorded tapes? I know I was a little late in giving them, but I did, didn't I?"

"The board no longer requires your services," she said coldly.

Before he could say another word, she fired. The bullet hit Clampton squarely in the chest. For a second, he stood still, stunned. He looked down at the red stain soaking his shirt, and then he fell to the ground.

David Clampton was dead.

"You didn't have to do that," Solaire said.

"You should worry about yourself, Mr. Solaire," she said, aiming the gun at him.

"What do you want?" Solaire asked.

"I want what you want."

"We didn't find it."

"Well, that is a shame," she said with a smirk. "Then you are no longer useful to me, either."

"We'll pay you double what they are paying you," Levack quickly said.

Solaire looked at him.

He shrugged. "It works in the movies."

"Maybe I'll shoot you first," she said, turning her gun to Levack.

"Let him go," Solaire said. "Your fight is with me."

She looked at him.

"I'm the one who broke into RBL. I'm the one who killed your men at the estate. I'm the one who was hired to find what Fisk was hiding. He had nothing to do with any of that."

"Then what is he? Your assistant?" she asked.

"More like a business acquaintance," Levack said.

"Just let him go," Solaire repeated.

"You know I can't do that, Mr. Solaire," she said. "You've put me in a difficult situation."

"Then shoot me first," Solaire said.

"Yeah, shoot him first," Levack said.

Solaire looked at him.

"Gotta extend my life as long as I can, buddy," Levack said.

Cain laughed. "Be careful who you choose as your friends, Mr. Solaire."

She aimed the gun at him.

"Be ready for the impact," Levack said to him. "It's going to be a blast."

He winked.

Solaire noticed something hidden in Levack's hand.

Before Cain could pull the trigger, there was a loud explosion that shook the walls of the storage unit. Then there was another, and another, the explosions coming in rapid succession.

The storage bin felt like it was going to tip over.

"Now," Levack yelled.

Solaire grabbed a lamp from a shelf and hurled it across at Cain. She ducked, and it flew over her head, but it hit the man behind her.

Before she could recover, Solaire rushed forward and shoved her hard with his shoulder. She fell to the floor, and her gun went flying in the air.

Without stopping, Solaire lunged at the man who had just been hit with the lamp.

Solaire kneed the man in the stomach. The man keeled over.

In the corner of his eye, he saw Levack punching the other man across the face.

Solaire thought about grabbing one of the weapons, but before he could, a bullet zipped past him.

Cain was still on the floor, but she had regained possession of her gun.

Solaire dashed down the row of units.

Another bullet flew past him and went straight into a wall.

Solaire reached the end and then quickly turned, his feet skidding on the floor.

Up ahead, he saw the freight elevator. He thought about taking it, but he knew there was no way he could wait for it. Instead, he turned right and headed for the stairs.

Another bullet zipped past him and hit a glass wall.

"Stop!" a voice boomed.

Solaire turned.

The man he had kneed was holding a gun, and it was aimed directly at him.

Cain appeared behind him.

She had a look of disdain on her face.

"This is the last time you'll be a thorn in my side," she spat. She leveled the gun at his head.

Suddenly there was a large explosion.

One of the storage bin's metal doors flew and hit the man squarely. The impact threw him hard into Cain.

The door landed on top of them both.

Solaire didn't hesitate for a second. He bolted through the doors and raced down the stairs.

In less than a minute, he was out the front door and running away from the self-storage building as fast as he could.

***

"You look like you've just gone through a boxing match," Humphries said.

Solaire was back at the pub. "And I'm guessing you didn't win," he added.

"Not quite."

"I know exactly what'll cheer you up." He went to the back and returned, holding a glass of iced tea. "Just the way you like it—no ice."

"Thank you," Solaire said.

When Solaire was halfway through his glass, he felt a man sit beside him.

"I'll have your hardest soda water that money can buy," Levack said.

"Coming right up," Humphries said. He came back with a glass and placed it before him.

Levack took a sip and made a face.

"Thanks," Solaire said, turning to him.

"For what?"

"For saving my life."

"I don't know what you're talking about," Levack said. "After I punched my guy, I ran as far away as I could."

*Of course, you did*, Solaire thought, knowing full well it was Levack who had detonated the last blast that hit Cain and her thug.

"Thanks anyway," Solaire said.

"Ah, don't mention it."

They both sat with their drinks for a moment before Levack said, "That was nice what you said back there."

"What?" Solaire turned to him.

"*Let him go*," Levack said. "It's nice to know there are still chivalric people out there."

"I knew it wasn't going to work, but it was worth a try."

"And it's the thought that counts," Levack said.

Solaire looked at the bottom of his glass. It was almost empty.

"What happens now?" Levack asked.

"I don't know." Solaire shook his head. "We were so close but so far."

"Is the mission over?"

"I don't know," Solaire said with a sigh. "I'm sure I'll be getting a call from Travers soon."

"What if it was there, but we failed to find it?" Levack said.

"In that case, the mission is definitely over."

"What are you going to do?" Levack asked.

"See if I can dig up some more leads or maybe even go back to Toronto."

"Yeah, it would be nice to go home."

"Where would that be?" Solaire turned to him.

Levack smiled. "Wouldn't you like to know?"

"One of these days, I'm going to make *you* my mission. Find out everything I need to know about you."

Levack laughed hard.

Solaire got up.

"Where are you going?" Levack asked.

"I think I better hit the sack."

"*Don't*. Even though we may not have succeeded in our mission, at least we succeeded in staying alive. That's something to celebrate."

Solaire thought for a moment and then said, "Fine."

"Great." Levack slapped him on the shoulder. "Another drink for my friend here," Levack yelled to Humphries.

"I have to make a pit stop," Solaire said.

"You mean go to the loo?"

Solaire smiled.

He walked to the end of the bar, turned right, and went down a hallway.

Up ahead, he saw both the men's and women's bathrooms.

As he was making his way there, he suddenly stopped.

In the middle of the hallway was a large board.

Photos were tacked on the board, probably of the pub's regular patrons. They consisted of various people, some on their wedding day, others on their skiing trips, and some smiling on the beach.

One, in particular, caught his attention.

He removed the picture from the board and stared at it.

His mouth nearly dropped.

He rushed back.

"That was quick," Levack said. "Your drink is waiting for you."

"No time," Solaire said, pulling out his cell phone. "We have to go."

"What?" Levack said, confused.

"I'll explain later."

Solaire began dialing numbers.

"Who're you calling?" Levack asked.

"Travers."

***

The car pulled up to the driveway.

A woman got out. She was carrying bags. She walked up the steps and then entered the cottage.

In the distance, hidden from view by trees and bushes, Solaire and Levack sat in the MINI Cooper, watching everything.

Solaire looked over at Levack.

"Let's do it," Levack said, putting the MINI in gear.

They drove up and parked behind the car.

They got out.

179

Levack touched his jacket pocket, feeling the gun.

"You won't need it," Solaire said.

"Just making sure," Levack said.

They went up the steps, and Solaire knocked on the door.

A moment later, the door swung open.

"Hello, Emma," Solaire said.

Emma Morgan's face turned pale.

"May we come in?" Solaire said.

Before she could answer, he pushed his way through.

"Who is it?" a voice asked from inside the house.

Two seconds later, Robbie Fisk emerged from down the hall.

"Hello, Mr. Fisk," Solaire said. "I'm not sure if you know me, but I know a lot about you."

***

They sat in the living room. Fisk and Emma were next to each other, and Solaire and Levack were across from them in separate chairs.

There was a chill in the air.

No one spoke until Emma finally said, "How did you find this place?"

Solaire pulled out a photo and placed it on the coffee table. "I found this at Humphries' pub." The photo showed Emma smiling in front of what looked like a cottage. "I saw this same cottage in another photo," Solaire continued. "It was during my conversation with Mrs. Fisk. In that photo, you, Mr. Fisk, were standing before it. You can imagine my surprise when I saw you, Emma, standing in front of one exactly like it."

Emma's head was down.

"I then started going over our conversations," Solaire said. "You once said that Mr. Fisk had not been seen in London. You were correct because he was outside of London. *Here*." Solaire moved his hands around the cottage. "And then at the party, you said Mr. Fisk *is* a good man, not that he *was* a good man, indicating that he was not dead but still alive. But I still wasn't sure until I listened to a recording that you, Mr. Fisk, had with a woman the day before your supposed suicide. That woman's voice was yours, Emma, so when I was certain there was a link between you and Mr. Fisk, I followed you here."

There was silence.

"For the past few days, I have been through quite an ordeal," Solaire said. "I have done things that may not be legal. I have taken actions that have caused a lot of damage, and on several occasions, I have even risked my own life. All this could have been avoided had I known the missing piece to all of it was still alive and living here. I expect an explanation, and I hope it's worth it."

"He's my father," Emma said.

Solaire's eyes narrowed.

"Yes," Fisk said. "Emma is my daughter. I didn't know until only a couple of months ago. I assure you, it came as a shock to me as well."

"You were the other woman everyone had been talking about?" Solaire asked.

Emma nodded.

"I didn't know what to do," Fisk said. "Except that I wanted to spend as much time as I could with her. I wanted to make up for lost time. She told me about what she and Sean did. SCABB became not only her passion but also mine. I wanted to do what was right."

"That was why RBL's board members thought you had started acting strange?" Solaire asked.

Fisk nodded. "Listen, I know I've made mistakes, but I wanted to rectify them. I tried making the other members listen to reason, but ultimately they were too blinded by greed. I figured I would use SCABB to get the point across."

"What about your apparent suicide?" Solaire asked.

"I had no choice," Fisk replied. "I was under surveillance. They had my phones tapped. I knew I had to do something, so one day I was driving to a meeting when I realized I was being followed. I called Emma and told her what was happening. That was when the plan was hatched. For a brief moment, I lost my tail, and that's when I put the car in gear and let it roll to the river. Emma was waiting for me in another car. She then drove me here."

"What about your stopover at the storage facility?"

"I had initially hidden the documents there, but when I knew I would have to disappear, I took them with me."

"Why hide?"

"At first I didn't know what to do. I thought about going to the authorities, but RBL's board members have friends all over London's high society. Then I found out a woman was looking for me."

"Claudia Cain," Solaire said.

"Is that her name?" Fisk asked. "Anyway, then Emma told me that someone was asking about RBL."

Solaire understood he was referring to him.

"Humphries is a friend of yours?" Solaire asked Emma.

"Yes," she replied. "When he told me about you, that's when I decided to get involved. At first, I didn't know if I could trust you, but now I know I can."

"Enough to still *not* tell me about your father?" Solaire shot back.

"It's not Emma's fault," Fisk said. "I told her not to do anything. She told me what happened to you at the estate. I wanted it to be safe—for her—before I took any actions."

"I can assure you it is safe now."

Fisk looked over at his daughter. She nodded.

He got up and left the room.

He returned with a portrait of the Queen.

From behind, he lifted a piece of cloth and pulled out a large envelope.

"This is what you've been searching for." He handed the envelope to Solaire. "Everything I found against the board members is in there."

Solaire felt the envelope. "There may be things you will have to answer for, too."

Fisk nodded. "I am ready for it." He smiled at his daughter.

Solaire and Levack got up.

"I'm sorry," Emma said. "I never meant for anything to happen to you."

"I know," Solaire said.

Solaire and Levack were heading to the door when Fisk asked, "Will you be able to bring down RBL?"

Solaire looked at him. "That's why I'm here."

***

He lay in bed, reading the morning newspaper.

He was in his flat in St. John's Wood.

Solaire had turned the page when he heard a knock at the door.

He answered. It was Travers.

They went to the living room.

"There is no mention of it in any of the newspapers," Solaire said, sitting down.

"We are trying to keep it like that for the next little while," Travers said, not taking a seat.

"Why?"

"RBL is too entrenched in London's society, so we have to be careful how we proceed. But I give you my word… Sir Blairwood, Lady Thatchburn, and Lord Cornell will be charged."

"What about Fisk?"

"We are keeping a close eye on him. No harm will come to him if that's what you are worried about. Right now, no one knows he is still alive, and we will keep it that way. He's our star witness, so we are going to take extra precautions to keep him safe."

"What about Emma?"

"There will be some scrutiny, but that will be from the media and not from us. She is not linked to RBL, so I don't see her getting involved in any way."

Solaire nodded but said nothing.

"You did a great job, Roman," Travers said. "CIL is grateful for everything you have done."

"Do they even know I exist?"

"No, but would you like them to?"

Solaire thought about it but then shook his head. "I guess if they knew, then I wouldn't be able to do my job the way I like to."

"Probably not."

Solaire stared out the window.

Travers looked around the flat. "You know you can afford better accommodations…"

"I know," Solaire replied.

"All right," Travers said. "I'll let you get some rest." He walked to the door. "But this rest will have to be short. We have a lot of work to do."


***


Solaire showered, changed, and went to a café.

He ordered a lemon pastry and a cup of tea.

When he was almost finished, a man came over and sat across from him.

"I'm famished, old chap," he said in a fake British accent.

Donald Levack had a large smile on his face.

"You're having a spot of tea?" Levack continued, still using the accent. "I think I will have that as well."

He waved the waiter over.

"I'll have three large eggs scrambled, two toasts with a side of mash potatoes, and your biggest sized cup of tea."

The waiter wrote it down but still gave Levack an odd look before going away.

"Should you not watch your weight at your age?" Solaire asked.

"My age?" Levack replied. "I'm a spry twenty-eight-year-old."

Solaire smiled. "I'm sure."

Levack's breakfast came, and he dug into it.

"What are your plans?" he asked.

"I'm going to stick around, maybe a day or two more. There are still parts of London I would like to see. What about you?"

"I'm going to Cleveland."

"Is that where you live?"

Levack looked at him and then nodded. "I've got someone waiting for me."

Solaire couldn't help but smile. This was the first time Levack had mentioned something personal about himself.

A car came up and stopped not too far from them.

Solaire got up. "Give them my regards, Donald."

"Where're you going?" Levack asked.

"There's someone who owes me one and would like to make it up to me."

Levack glanced at the waiting car.

Behind the wheel was Emma Morgan.

Levack smiled. "You devil, you."

"I don't know London too well, so I need a tour guide."

"I'm sure you do." Levack was still smiling.

"Goodbye, Donald," Solaire said, walking away. "Have a safe trip back."

"Maybe I'll see you in another city," Levack yelled back.

Solaire turned and smiled. "You can count on it."

***

Solaire got in the car.
Emma kissed him.
"What was that for?" he asked.
She smiled. "Gratitude for all you did."
Solaire smiled and kissed her back.

# The Paradise Gallery

THE HAGUE

"Your man was brilliant in London," the Dutchman said.

"Bloody marvelous indeed," the Englishman said.

Travers merely smiled.

The Dutchman said, "Your report is nothing short of extraordinary."

The Englishman said, "I would love to shake your man's hand."

"I'll make sure to pass your compliments on to him," Travers said.

"You must at least tell us his name," the Dutchman said.

Travers shook his head. "It would be better if you didn't know."

"This man deserves recognition—a medal, in fact," the Englishman said.

"I'm sure he'll be grateful for the accolades, but his identity must remain a secret—for now," Travers said.

The Dutchman glared at him. "While I fully appreciate the difficult task we have placed on you, you have to realize that we have responsibilities of our own as well."

"I understand them," Travers said.

"The Judge has asked about him," the Englishman said.

"She has?" Travers raised an eyebrow in surprise.

"The reports that you provide go directly to her, and she is very impressed."

"I am honored that she is satisfied with our results, but I respectfully say that I still cannot reveal who he is."

Both the Dutchman and the Englishman were silent.

"As you wish," the Dutchman finally said. "You have your next assignment."

"I do, and I have already sent my man there."


MONTREAL

Roman Solaire held his breath and went down deep into the water. He came up for air and then freestyled down the length of the pool.

Among many other amenities, Hotel Le Crystal had an indoor pool. This morning it was empty, allowing Solaire complete and undisturbed access.

The mission in London had taken a mental toll on him, not to mention his body. The saltwater was the perfect remedy for healing cuts and bruises.

He completed ten laps and then emerged from the water.

He dried himself with a towel and put on a bathrobe.

He took an elevator to the eleventh floor.

The Penthouse Suite was everything anyone could ask for. It had a separate living room, two bathrooms, a bedroom with a king-size bed, and a workspace with a desk and chair.

Solaire ordered breakfast.

While he waited, he strolled to the spacious terrace. The morning sky was clear, giving him a perfect view of Mount Royal. Below he could see that downtown Montreal was beginning to get busy with commuters.

He took a deep breath. It felt both refreshing and exhilarating.

He heard a knock at the door.

A man wearing the hotel's uniform was waiting with a cart.

"Where would you like it, sir?" the man politely asked.

"Outside, please."

The man rolled the cart to the terrace.

Solaire thanked and tipped him, and the man left.

Solaire sat on the deck chair and took a bite of the warm, buttered croissant. He washed the bite down with a hot cup of espresso.

From the cart, Solaire picked up two newspapers: *The Globe and Mail* and *La Presse*. Solaire placed the latter aside. His French was not what it used to be, and attempting to read the news in French would only confuse him further.

Solaire was born not far from Montreal to a French father and an English mother. But before he started school, his mother moved him to Toronto, and thus he missed the opportunity to learn the language at the developmental stage.

The only French he heard was from his father, who made sure to speak to him in his native tongue.

Solaire scanned the first pages of the *Globe*, which included reports on student protests, union strikes, and even a gruesome murder.

He flipped through the pages and then stopped.

A politician was again raising the issue of why the province of Quebec should separate from the rest of Canada. The politician, born and raised in Eastern Quebec, was a hard-line "sovereigntist" or "separatist." He believed an independent Quebec was the only alternative for the survival of the Francophone culture.

Solaire found this troubling. He always viewed Quebec as the heart of Canada. Just look at the map, he would say. Quebec was to the left side of the country, where a heart would be in a human body. Remove the heart, and the body dies. Remove Quebec, and Canada will not survive.

Solaire slapped the newspaper shut and put it aside.

He was proud that his father was a Francophone and his mother, an Anglophone. He was a proud Quebecer and a proud Canadian. He felt he had gotten the best of both worlds.

Canada needed Quebec, and Quebec needed Canada. That's the way he saw it.

There was a knock at the front door, breaking his thoughts.

He got up and answered.

The same man who had earlier brought him his breakfast was now holding a white envelope.

"This came for you, sir."

Solaire thanked him, closed the door, and then tore the envelope open.

Inside was a handwritten note.

*Dear RS,*

*Please meet me at 10:00 am at the Kondiaronk Belvedere on Mount Royal.*


*CT*


Solaire knew who the sender was.

Solaire glanced at the clock. He had more than enough time.

He showered, shaved, and put on a gray sweatshirt, black jeans, and slip-on walking shoes.

He then checked himself in the mirror.

The bruises from his last mission had all but healed. Except for some tiny red marks, there would be no permanent scarring.

Satisfied, he left his room.

***


The view of downtown Montreal from Mount Royal was picturesque. An early morning fog hung over the buildings, with the hope that the sun would eventually break through.

The "lookout," as the locals liked to call it, was already filled with people. He spotted people walking, jogging, and cycling. Tourists and locals lined up along the edge, snapping photographs. Two elderly individuals were practicing what looked like yoga or tai-chi, not too far from him.

Solaire felt someone standing next to him.

He turned to find Clive Travers staring at the city.

Solaire said, "If I were you, I would get my camera out and take a picture."

"Beautiful indeed," Travers said. "But, I think I'll get a postcard instead."

"When did you arrive in Montreal?" Solaire asked.

"Recently."

Solaire already knew getting direct answers from Travers was never easy.

"Did you do any sightseeing?" Solaire asked.

"Not yet, but I'm hoping to once we are done here."

Solaire waited.

"Before we begin," Travers said, "my employers are very pleased with you. One would even like to shake your hand."

"Is that so?" Solaire raised an eyebrow.

"Both New York and London were outstanding successes. I can't tell you how much credibility it has given CIL in the international community."

"I'm glad I can be of some service to the Court of International Law."

"You have been more than that, Roman," Travers said, correcting him. "In fact, you have put CIL in a position where other countries are now seeking our assistance. CIL can and will prosecute those who are affecting international stability."

"Who's affecting international stability in Montreal?" Solaire asked.

From underneath his jacket, Travers pulled out a legal-size envelope and handed it to him.

Solaire extracted two small black and white photos.

The first was of a man in his early to late forties—slim and short with salt-and-pepper hair. The man was wearing a dark, fitted suit.

"Julian Barthez," Travers said. "Have you heard of him?"

Solaire pondered the question. "The name sounds familiar."

"It should. In the nineties, Barthez was one of the hottest young entrepreneurs in North America. He graduated from McGill University, specializing in computer programming. He quickly landed in Silicon Valley, where he started an internet company. That company grew from two people to over a hundred employees. Several big companies tried to buy it out, and there were rumors that one even made an offer of over one hundred million dollars. But Barthez held firm. He believed the company was going to explode and one day be able to buy those very same companies that wanted to buy them. But then the dot com crash happened, and the company went bankrupt. Investors lost millions of dollars. Naturally, they blamed Barthez. Had he sold the company, they would have not only recouped their investment but also made extra on top."

Solaire nodded. "I remember reading that."

"Barthez became a pariah in the industry. No one wanted to get near him or invest in his ventures, for that matter. He soon disappeared and was not heard from until recently."

Solaire listened intently.

"Have you heard of CTS?" Travers asked.

Solaire shook his head.

"Cloud Tracking System is a company that is developing or has already developed a software application that, when installed, can track just about anything. For instance, it can tell who is doing what on a specific computer, or which location a certain vehicle is in, or even who is watching what shows at any particular time."

Solaire was confused. "Don't they already have programs to track those? I mean, anyone can remotely access someone's computer, a GPS can track where someone is driving to or from, and even which shows the population is watching and at what time."

"Yes, but no single application can track *everything*."

Solaire went silent.

"Imagine you wanted to know who's doing what in the office, or what programs your children are watching, or how long it'll take your wife to get home. You can do all that *simultaneously* on your phone. The key behind the application is that it'll attach itself to any program and extrapolate the requested data."

"Ingenious," Solaire said.

"Yes, but in the wrong hands, it can be highly dangerous."

Solaire waited for more.

Travers said, "After the dot com crash, no one wanted to invest in any of Barthez's ventures, so he has found private investors from all over the world. Our source tells us the investors have links to Iran, North Korea, and even China. With money coming in from those countries, who's to say the information will not be passed to them?"

"What you are saying is that it can be used for spying," Solaire finally said. "Then why doesn't the Canadian government just stop Barthez?"

"On what basis?" Travers said. "CTS is developing an application that *can* be used by the general public for their own benefit. CTS has assured all government agencies that it doesn't collect any data or store it. But we have reason to believe otherwise."

"How?"

"I know I said we have a source, but what I should say is, we *had* a source. Pierre Gauthier was found dead in his home, which he shared with his wife and two children.'"

"Are you sure he's dead? You know what happened in London."

"I know, and yes, he is dead. His wife discovered the body, and there is even a coroner's report."

"How did he die?" Solaire asked.

"That's the problem. We don't know," Traver's replied. "The coroner's report shows death by heart failure, which is unusual because Gauthier was not even forty. He jogged every morning, and there are no known heart issues in the family. It was as if one day he just died."

"You think Barthez had something to do with it?"

"I don't know, but it seems like more than a coincidence that around the time we were informed of what CTS was working on, our informant suddenly and inexplicably dropped dead."

Solaire flipped over to the second black and white photograph.

It was of a man, extremely large, with a slicked ponytail and a stylish goatee.

"Marcel," Travers said. "He accompanies Barthez everywhere he goes. He may be far more menacing than he looks, but this I cannot confirm. Just be careful."

"I always am," Solaire said, touching the marks on his face.

"CTS has provided the application to a number of companies in order for the beta users to help identify any kinks it may have. I hear that so far, there were no issues found, which means the application may be rolled out soon across the board. I also hear that the Canadian government is interested in the application. This can have dramatic effects on your country's national security if that were to happen. As per Gauthier, we know CTS is storing the data from the application, even if they claim otherwise." Travers turned to Solaire. "Roman, we need to find where they are holding this information. If we can do that, then we can not only charge Barthez with providing information to dangerous individuals and regimes, we can also stop the application from spreading."

Solaire looked across at the buildings. The fog had disappeared, and the sun was now shining brightly on the city of Montreal.

"All right," he finally said.

***

Solaire returned to his suite and pulled out his laptop.

He spent the better part of the morning researching CTS.

There wasn't much information online. CTS was still private and wasn't obligated to reveal their operations to the public, but he did find something interesting on Barthez.

Barthez was an avid art collector. Before the dot com crash, he had amassed a collection that included a Rembrandt, a Picasso, an Andy Warhol, and even a Van Gogh. After the crash, Barthez was forced to sell—if not all, then most of his prized possessions. Now he collected artwork by local or emerging artists.

Solaire spotted one article and clicked on it.

Barthez had recently purchased several pieces of artwork from a boutique gallery. Solaire clicked on their About Us link. A photo of a woman appeared. Solaire raised an eyebrow. She was stunning. She had long, dark brown hair, emerald green eyes, and she wore a tight red dress. Underneath the photo was her name, Sophie Paradis, and she was the owner and curator of the Paradise Gallery.

Solaire leaned back in his chair.

*Maybe later today, I will pay Ms. Paradis a visit*, he thought.

***

Solaire took a taxi to an address in Saint-Henri. What he saw before him did not look like a software company that was developing a sophisticated computer application. It was a run-down building with boarded-up windows and doors. The paint had long since faded, and graffiti covered much of the walls.

Solaire looked down the street. All the buildings were in a similar state or worse.

Solaire should have become suspicious when after hearing the address, the taxi driver gave him an odd look.

Solaire now wished he hadn't sent the taxi driver away.

He looked around again and saw no one nearby.

*Well, I am already here, so why not check it out*? he thought.

He examined the wooden board nailed over what used to be a door. He found an opening, eased his fingers in between, and pried the wood back.

He entered the building.

It was dark and damp.

As he proceeded further, he noticed a light coming through the back windows, which were not boarded.

The interior was in a horrid state. There were holes the size of basketballs in the walls. Materials were hanging from the high ceilings, including light fixtures. The floor was covered in dirt and debris.

Solaire nearly hit a desk, which upon deeper inspection was missing its legs. There were broken tables and chairs, balls of mangled wires, and even computer equipment scattered here and there.

Solaire's booted foot hit a cardboard box. He pushed it over with his foot. Binders and other reading materials poured out.

Solaire examined them. There was no indication of whom they belonged to.

Solaire did a three-sixty scan of the surroundings. Satisfied there was nothing of importance to be found, he left.

Outside he took a deep breath of fresh air.

He pulled out the cell phone given to him by Travers. He dialed a number.

"Yes," Travers answered.

"You gave me the wrong address," Solaire fumed. "CTS is not here."

"That can't be right," Travers said. "Our source was certain of the location."

"The only thing certain is that the building is vacant and has been for some time."

Travers repeated the address.

"Yes, and there is nothing here."

"I am sorry, Roman," Travers said. "Pierre Gauthier provided us this address. As he is no longer alive to confirm or deny this, you are on your own. I trust your ability to find it."

The line went dead.

Solaire shoved the phone back in his pocket.

He looked around. The streets were empty. He decided to walk to the main road. Maybe there he'd be able to find another taxi.

When he was behind the building, he stopped. Near the back door was a blue piece of paper.

Upon picking it up, he realized it was a plastic sticker. A section of it was torn off, but Solaire could make out the name of the company.

Solaire had an idea.

***

He stood in front of Leblanc & Leblanc Movers.

The building was surrounded by a ten-foot chain-link fence. Solaire counted nine large moving trucks and vans in the front.

He went inside.

Behind the counter was a pale girl with light blue eyes.

"*Bonjour*," she said with a smile.

"Hello," he said. "I wonder if you can help me."

Solaire hoped she spoke English, or else he would have to resort to his broken French.

To his relief, she said, "I will try."

Solaire noticed that when the sun hit her eyes, the blue became even lighter.

"I had left my cat with my friend, and when I returned, he had moved away. I was hoping you could tell me where he moved so I can pick her up."

"My manager is not here," the girl said. "I can call him and find out if we are allowed to give that information."

"Why bother him for something this small?" Solaire asked, softening his voice. "I would call my friend, but his cell phone is not working, and his telephone number from the old address is no longer in service.

The girl bit her bottom lip. "I don't know."

"I haven't seen Celine in weeks," Solaire said.

"Celine?"

"That's my cat's name."

"It's such a sweet name," the girl said.

"It would be even sweeter if I could see her again." Solaire was almost pleading.

The girl looked at him and then asked, "What was the address?"

Solaire gave the address in Saint-Henri.

The girl checked the computer and gave another address. This one was in centre-ville.

***

Solaire stood in front of the building. It was granite and reached at least twenty floors.

He entered through the revolving doors and was in the front lobby.

He approached the building directory on the wall and searched up and down.

He glanced at the piece of paper the girl had given him and then up at the directory again.

The ninth floor was for Direct Logistics Inc., not CTS.

He had hoped the moving company would be the link to finding where CTS might be located. But this was not the case.

He spotted a fast food restaurant opposite the building.

Throughout the day, he hadn't had time to eat anything, and now his stomach was beginning to grumble.

He crossed the street and entered the restaurant.

He ordered a large bowl of poutine, which was essentially French fries covered in brown gravy and cheese curds.

He found a seat near the windows and began devouring his meal.

It had been many years since he had poutine, and now he remembered why he loved it. He had tried something similar in other countries, but it did not compare to the way the French-Canadians made it.

He was almost at the bottom of the bowl when he noticed something.

A large man in a black suit came out of the building that Solaire had just been in.

Solaire immediately recognized him.

It was Marcel, Barthez's bodyguard.

Marcel walked along the side of the building and then disappeared in the back.

Solaire rushed out of the restaurant and, within seconds, had crossed the street.

The back of the building was a parking lot, and it was entirely filled with cars.

Solaire walked past the rows of cars, but he could not find Marcel.

He retreated to the front of the building, passed the revolving doors, and was in the lobby again.

He took the elevator up.

On the ninth floor, he was confronted with a closed door that had a sign plate with the words *Direct Logistics Inc.* on it.

Solaire was certain CTS was behind that door. Now, if he could only gain access to make sure.

There was a card reader next to the door.

Solaire thought about procuring an access card from any of the employees that were bound to come out, but he didn't want to raise any alarms.

*I will have to find another way in*, he thought.

***

Solaire headed back to the hotel, but first, he stopped at a printing shop.

Back in his room, he changed into a white dress shirt, beige dress pants, and black dress shoes. He pulled on a blue blazer and then left.

The Paradise Gallery was located in *Vieux-Montreal* or Old Montreal.

There were several paintings displayed near the front windows.

Solaire entered.

He could tell the gallery was small, but with the high ceilings and open spaces, it looked bigger.

He saw a man and a woman placing a frame on a wall.

Once the woman spotted him, she immediately came over.

"*Bonjour*," she said with a smile. "*Soyez bienvenus à la Galerie de Paradis*." Solaire understood that she had welcomed him to the Paradise Gallery, but he hesitated in speaking to her in French, out of fear, there might be some things lost in translation.

"Thank you," he said.

Her smile widened. She was even more stunning in person, and Solaire had to control himself from staring at her.

"Welcome," she said in her French accent. "My name is Sophie, and this is my gallery."

"I see you have some wonderful pieces here," Solaire said.

"Is there something specific you are looking for?" she asked.

"No. I scour local art establishments in search of something that will blow me away, as they say. Oh, how rude of me…" Solaire put his hand in his blazer pocket and pulled out his card.

"Roman Solaire," she said, reading the card aloud. "Travers Private Art Collections."

"My business is uniting clients with pieces of art that were made just for them."

"Really?" she said, revealing perfect white teeth. "I'm sure we have many pieces that your clients will enjoy owning. But I must warn you, our collection isn't… how you say, very pricey. We feature mostly works by local artists, and some of them are my friends."

"I completely understand," Solaire said. "If I wanted pricey, I would have gone to Christie's. I have an eclectic list of clients whose tastes vary from one to the other. These clients are art connoisseurs, so they do appreciate art for art's sake, not for any monetary value it may hold."

"That is good to hear," she said. "Let me show you around."

They walked around the gallery, stopping at each piece of work. Sophie explained the history behind the work, including who the artist was and how it could fit into someone's collections.

Solaire nodded and occasionally smiled. In reality, he didn't really appreciate art. He felt it was pretentious. He never understood how people could spend millions, and in some cases, hundreds of millions on a single piece of artwork, while there were millions of people starving in the world. In some ways, it felt like the industry was self-indulgent.

As they moved from one piece to another, he found the paintings to be more and more obscure. One was completely baffling because it had nothing but a single tiny dot in the middle of a large white canvas.

Solaire leaned closer, hoping the dot would reveal something of significance, but it didn't.

It would be entirely incorrect to say Solaire hated art. He admired realistic painters. He was fond of works by Canadian wildlife artist Robert Bateman. As a kid, his family had dining table placemats with Bateman's paintings on them. He clearly remembered eating his cereal while a Bengal tiger stared at him from underneath the bowl.

They were at the end of the tour when Solaire said, "Thank you, Ms. Paradis, for taking the time to show me around."

"Call me, Sophie," she said. "Can I ask if anything blew you away?" From her voice, it sounded like she was hoping that Solaire would buy a piece.

Solaire looked around. "I can't say it did."

"Well, I have good news for you," she said. "We have many more wonderful works that you can look through in our catalog."

Solaire looked at his watch. "I'm sorry, but I'm afraid I have another engagement later today."

She looked disappointed, but she kept up her smile.

"I have an idea," Solaire said. "I'm only here in Montreal for a few days. Tomorrow night, why don't I take you out to dinner, and perhaps you can show me the catalog then."

"Yes, I would love that!"

"Well, then, I'll see you tomorrow."

Roman Solaire left the Paradise Gallery utterly relieved that Sophie Paradis had not turned him down.

***

Solaire walked down Old Montreal. The sun had come down, and the streets were now illuminated by streetlamps.

The cobblestone lanes and architecture made it look like he was back in seventeenth-century France.

When Solaire passed by City Hall, he stopped.

On the side wall of the building was a graffiti-style painting. Solaire leaned closer and examined it.

The outline was shaped in a square with the interior painted in bright yellow. Inside the square was a woman on her knees, praying. The woman was drawn in great detail.

Solaire continued walking.

When he passed Bonsecours Market, he stopped once again.

There was another painting on the side of another building. This time the outline was a triangle. The inside was colored in bright blue with a detailed drawing of a boy in his bed praying.

Solaire didn't know what to make of it.

A young couple stopped and began taking photos of the painting.

Solaire moved down the street.

Behind him, in the distance, he heard a noise.

Solaire paid no attention to it.

The sound became louder.

People turned and looked in its direction. Solaire did so, too.

A single headlight flashed his way. Solaire squinted to see what it was. A man wearing a black leather jacket, a black bandana, and dark sunglasses was riding an oversize Harley Davidson.

The motorcycle was half a block away.

Not making much of it, Solaire kept going.

He had not even taken twenty steps when he realized the motorcycle had not passed by him.

He turned and found the Harley a three-car length behind him. It was going at a slow but steady pace.

Solaire had a sinking feeling that he was being followed.

He quickened his steps.

At the end of the block, he turned right.

To his horror, he saw the single ominous light also turn into his street.

Solaire began to jog.

Suddenly, from behind him, the roar of the motorcycle became loud. The Harley had come to life.

Solaire spotted another turn. He took it.

He was now in a narrow lane. Without pausing, he rushed forward, his feet pounding on the cobblestone.

There was a turn up ahead. When he came around it, he was confronted with a wall.

It was a dead end.

Solaire retreated but stopped when he heard footsteps.

He now regretted not entering any one of the restaurants he had run past.

Solaire searched and found a piece of two-by-four wood.

He held it firmly in his hands.

He controlled his breathing in order to listen clearly.

The footsteps were approaching fast.

He braced himself.

Just when the rider turned the corner, Solaire swung the piece of wood at his head.

It connected with the rider's forehead.

The rider fell back, clutching his face.

Solaire dropped the piece of wood and, without another glance at the rider, ran through the narrow lane.

When he was at the end, he heard a familiar voice cry, "Roman!"

Solaire stopped and turned to face Donald Levack.

Levack was middle-aged and slightly overweight with green eyes. His dark glasses were on the ground in two pieces.

"Aw, you broke them," Levack said, picking them up.

Solaire had met Levack on his previous missions. Levack had, on occasion, saved his life.

Solaire walked up to him. "You're lucky I didn't break *you*. Why are you dressed like that?" Solaire eyed him up and down.

"What? You mean this?" Levack tugged at his leather jacket. "All the locals wear them."

"No, they do not," Solaire said. "You look like a member of Hells Angels."

Levack's face had a blank look.

"They are a notorious biker gang, unpopular with the Royal Canadian Mounted Police."

"Oh." Levack's face flushed. "I was wondering why people were giving me dirty looks."

They walked down the narrow lane.

Solaire saw the Harley. "Where did you pick it up?"

"It's a rental," Levack said, holding his head. "I wanted to blend in."

"You're lucky the real Hells Angels didn't catch you."

Levack rubbed his forehead. "Is it bad? Will my wife notice it?"

"You're married?" Solaire said, raising an eyebrow. "The things I learn about you when I visit different cities."

Levack shrugged. "You were bound to find out anyway. What's the damage?"

Solaire examined him. "It looks quite nasty, actually. I think we should take you to the emergency room."

"Really?" Levack looked worried.

"Yes, but I hope you have hitman insurance."

Levack relaxed. "I didn't know you had a sense of humor."

Solaire said, "I guess we both learn something new when we visit different countries. Come, I know a place around the corner where we can get some drinks."

"I hope you remember I've been sober for over eight years now."

"I do, and I wouldn't want you to start drinking now," Solaire said. "My offer is for non-alcoholic drinks, of course."

Levack nodded. "I think I better take these off." He pulled off the bandana and the leather jacket.

"It's a good idea, considering we are going to a place owned by the Hells Angels." Solaire laughed.

"Funny," Levack said as they walked down the street. "I think I preferred the dull and boring Roman Solaire."

***

The next morning, Solaire sat on the balcony of his hotel room reading the *Globe and Mail.* His breakfast consisted of eggs on an English biscuit, hash browns on the side, and a pastry. He rinsed the meal down with a cup of black coffee.

Solaire had a long day ahead of him, so he thought he might as well stuff up now.

When Solaire was almost to the end of the *Globe*, there was a knock at the door.

He answered. It was Levack.

Unlike yesterday, Levack was wearing a dark blue jacket over a green golf shirt, with black pants and black shoes.

"Wow." Levack looked around the Penthouse suite. "They do take care of you."

"Where are you staying?" Solaire asked.

"Ah, some dump in a questionable neighborhood. There is no hot water, and the toilet doesn't flush right. But I do get fifteen channels on my black and white TV."

Solaire knew Levack was joking. One thing he had learned by now was that both Travers and Levack never gave a straight answer.

Maybe that was how all spies or government agents worked. Information was power, and they kept it close to their chests, even when dealing with fellow agents or coworkers. There was always a chance one of them could turn to the enemy's side. Better to be safe than dead.

"Can I order you breakfast?" Solaire said.

Levack tapped his protruding belly. "I already ate, but what are you having?"

Solaire told him.

"All right, but skip the hash browns. I gotta maintain my handsome physique."

When Levack was done, he let out a loud burp.

"*Pardon moi*," he said, imitating a fake French accent. "De meal was de-*licious*."

Solaire said nothing. He just looked over the balcony at the sprawling city below.

"What's the plan?" Levack said. "Cause I came prepared." He pulled up his jacket, and Solaire spotted a firearm.

"You know I don't like guns."

"Yeah, I know, but I love 'em. I don't leave home without a pair of washed underwear and my little friend here."

"I'm hoping this time we won't need to resort to that level of violence."

"Remember London?" Levack said.

Solaire touched his left eyebrow. He shook his head and turned to Levack. "I believe I have found where CTS is located."

"Great!" Levack clapped his hands. "Let's go nail these suckers."

"Not so fast," Solaire said. "We first need to gain access to this location without being detected. We don't want to alarm Barthez. We already know what they are developing…"

"The application," Levack interjected.

"Precisely. What we need to find is where they are storing the data accumulated from the application."

"And you don't think it's at CTS?"

Solaire shook his head. "They are assuring their clients that no data is kept by CTS, and they would be risking it if they received a surprise visit by any of their clients. I believe it is somewhere else."

"How're we going to find it?"

"I'm not sure. I am hoping that once we are inside CTS, we will find something that'll lead us to it."

"We're pretty much going in there with blind hope?" Levack asked.

Solaire didn't have an answer.

Levack said, "Why don't we just follow Barthez to where he's keeping this data? He's got to go there once in a while."

"I thought about that, but Barthez is too smart. He knows the data can be stored in a remote location without the need for his constant supervision. He may already have technicians keeping an eye on them."

"Then why don't we find these technicians and follow them?"

Solaire gave him a look.

"Oh, yeah," Levack said, almost slapping his forehead. "If we already knew who the technicians were, then we would have already found the location, right?"

"Right."

"Okay, we go with your plan." Levack stood up. "Let's go visit CTS."

***

Solaire waited across the street. He was back in centre-ville, but this time with Levack, who was in the CTS building.

Twenty minutes later, Levack came out and approached him.

"What did you find out?" Solaire asked.

"His name his Dominique Roy," Levack replied. "He will be on shift tonight."

They already knew the name of the company that provided cleaning services for the CTS building. Now they knew who they had to approach to gain access to it.

***

"Are you sure this is the right address?" Solaire asked, looking up at the apartment building.

They were in Griffintown, a neglected neighborhood south of Montreal.

"That's what the guy in the building told me," Levack replied.

"I am curious as to how he gave you this information," Solaire said.

Levack leaned in and winked. "I have my ways, and don't worry, I didn't even have to pull out my special friend." Levack tugged at his jacket.

They took the stairs up and stopped on the third floor. They knocked at a door.

A woman answered.

She was plump and stocky with freckles all over her face and body.

"Hello," Solaire said. "Does a Dominique Roy live here?" Solaire knew Griffintown was a predominately Irish neighborhood, so he hoped the woman spoke English, or else he'd have to revert to French.

The woman eyed them both. "Yes, but what's this about?"

"It's better if we speak to him," Solaire said.

"I don't know. Dom's sleeping."

"Do you mind waking him? It's important," Solaire said.

She still didn't move. She crossed her arms. "I ain't going anywhere unless you tell me why you're here."

Solaire was about to say something when Levack spoke up, "Listen, lady. Go in there and wake your man up." Levack opened his jacket, revealing his gun. "If you don't, then I'll go and wake him up myself, but then I won't guarantee he'll stay awake after I'm done with him."

The woman turned pale and then disappeared.

Solaire looked at him.

Levack shrugged. "Sometimes, you gotta talk *their* talk."

A man came out. He was unshaven and balding, with wisp of hair flying here and there.

"What can I do for you?" he said, blinking.

"Mr. Roy," Solaire said, "we are from the Casino de Montreal. We understand you are a regular there."

Roy's eyes widened. He turned and closed the door to the apartment. "My wife doesn't need to know this."

"That is exactly why we preferred to speak to you directly. We know you owe quite a bit of money to the casino."

"And I'm going to pay it, I swear." Roy lifted his hand up.

"Please remind us how much it is that you owe," Solaire said.

"Fourteen hundred bucks," Roy said.

"That's quite a bit of money," Solaire said, turning to Levack.

"Indeed, it is. Enough for someone to have their legs broken."

"But—" Solaire turned to Roy again. "You are in luck."

"I am?" Roy said, confused.

"Yes, we need your help. In return, we will give you the fourteen hundred dollars to repay the casino."

"We will?" Levack said, confused.

"Yes, we will. But we need you to do something for us."

Roy's face brightened up. "Yeah, anything."

"We need you to not go into work today."

***

The sun was coming down when Solaire entered the CTS building wearing a cleaning service uniform. It was Roy's, but at least it fit—in most places.

The security guard at the front desk looked at him.

"Where's Dom?" he asked.

"I don't know, but my supervisor told me to come down."

"Can I see your ID?" the guard asked.

Solaire handed it to him. It was Roy's but with Solaire's photo and name on it.

"Bind. Jim Bind?"

"Yes, that's me."

The guard looked at Solaire and then at the card. "All right. Do you know what to do?"

"It's my job." Solaire gave him a smile. "Just point me to where the supplies are."

"Level B1, on your right."

"Thanks." Solaire headed for the elevators.

Solaire grabbed the cleaning cart and headed straight for the ninth floor. He stopped in front of Direct Logistics Inc.

He scanned Roy's card, but instead of the light turning green, it stayed red. He scanned the card again and again. The doors did not open.

Solaire was certain Roy would have access to all the floors and units.

He then had an idea. He quickly looked through the cleaning products in the cart. Most, if not all, were eco-friendly products. Ones that if drunk by accident, would not cause permanent damage to the drinker.

Solaire pulled out a pen, filled the cap with the liquid from one of the cleaners, and sealed it with tape. He now had a laxative.

He then took the elevator down to the ground floor.

He placed the cleaning cart to the side, removed the bucket and mop, and began polishing the floor.

He worked his way around the floor until he reached the security guard's desk.

The guard was busy reading a sports magazine. He had his feet up, and he was leaning back in his chair. He made no effort to engage Solaire in any way.

When Solaire passed him, in one quick motion, he poured the liquid from the cap into the guard's coffee mug.

He then moved away.

He continued mopping, but this time at a much slower pace.

Not even twenty minutes had gone by when the guard immediately got up and ran toward the bathroom.

Solaire dropped the mop and rushed to the guard's desk.

Earlier, when he had first met the guard, he had seen a set of keys and passes on the desk. Solaire hoped that the guard had left them behind in a hurry.

He had.

Solaire grabbed them, and after collecting everything in the cart, he took the elevator back to the ninth floor.

He scanned the guard's card, and this time the light turned green. The door unlocked.

Solaire pulled the door open, placed the cleaning cart in between, so it didn't shut, then took the elevator back to the ground floor.

The desk was still empty.

Solaire returned the keys and passes from where he'd found them and then went back up.

***

Solaire entered the office. The room contained rows upon rows of cubicles with laptops and desktop computers.

Solaire was not completely sure if it was CTS or, in fact, Digital Logistics Inc., as the name on the door had indicated.

He was going based on his instincts. If Travers was correct about the address in Saint-Henri, then the moving company records would indicate that they had moved to this location.

He peered into the cubicles hoping to find some sign that this was CTS. But he found none.

Any documents he picked up contained the header DLI.

Solaire passed a room. He stopped and then entered. It looked like a boardroom. It had a large table in the middle with chairs around it. Around the walls were white writing boards with all forms of codes, numbers, letters, acronyms, and even flow charts. None of it made any sense to Solaire, though. He might as well have been reading a foreign language. Either this was a code for the application or for some human resources program.

Solaire left the room.

He looked around and found the main office. It was locked.

He searched each cubicle and returned with two hairpins.

He examined the lock, and then using the hairpins, he raked it until he heard a *click*. The lock was broken.

He entered.

The room was small, with a desk and chair in the middle.

There were no cabinets, shelves, or other items.

Solaire placed himself behind the desk but found there was no computer, just a cord for where a laptop would be.

He pulled the drawers open but found nothing of importance, only writing materials.

He locked the room and then left Digital Logistics Inc.

He took the elevator down. The security guard was still behind his desk, but instead of reading his magazine, he had his head down as if he were in considerable pain.

Solaire waited until the guard hurriedly got up and left the desk.

Solaire rushed to the front, unlocked the door, and left the building.

Across the street, he met Levack.

"What did you find?" Levack asked.

"Nothing." Solaire shook his head. "The excursion was a waste."

"What do we do now?"

"I don't know," Solaire said as he moved away.

"Where are you going?" Levack asked.

"I have to meet someone for dinner."

***

She looked stunning, even in the low light.

Solaire was escorted to a table near the windows.

Sophie Paradis smiled once she saw him.

"Sorry I'm late," he said, sitting opposite her.

"It's okay. I've only been here a couple of minutes."

"Splendid choice," Solaire said, looking around.

The restaurant had a modern look to it but an old-fashioned feel. The walls were metallic with water trickling down, giving the place a futuristic design, but the lamps with their yellow shades of light gave it a homely ambiance.

It felt like a fusion between the new and the old.

The waiter came over. "Welcome, Madam, and Monsieur. My name is François, and I'll be your waiter today. May I interest you in a bottle of wine?"

"Nothing for me, just water," Solaire said. "But, the lady may like some."

"What do you recommend?" she said to the waiter.

"Madam, I'll get you our special of the day." The waiter left.

"You don't drink?" Sophie said.

Solaire shook his head. "I have a sensitive stomach."

"What do you drink?"

"You'll laugh if I told you."

"Try me." She looked at him intently.

"Iced tea without the ice."

Her eyebrows arched. "How interesting, but why no ice?"

"It dilutes the flavor."

She nodded.

"Tell me a little bit about yourself," Solaire said.

"What would you like to know?"

"Where were you born? How did you end up owning an art gallery?"

"I was born in Quebec City but raised in Montreal. I went to McGill University, studying art history. During that time, I started working for a local gallery here. It was then that I realized how much I loved doing it. It enabled me to bring together both the art creator and the art consumer. I was the bridge between both worlds. After getting my bachelor's, I went abroad to London."

"I was just there."

"Really?" Her eyes lit up. "Isn't it a wonderful place?"

"Yes, quite." Solaire wasn't about to tell her that he barely made it out alive.

The waiter returned with a bottle of wine and poured some in a glass for her. He placed a glass of water before Solaire. He handed them menus. "I will be back to take your orders." He left.

"Please continue," Solaire said.

"In London, I received my master's in art business from Sotheby's Institute of Art."

"I didn't know the auction house had a school."

"Yes, and also one in New York."

"Prior to London, I was also in New York," Solaire said.

"I've only been there once but would like to go regularly. It's a great city, isn't it?"

"It absolutely is." Solaire took a sip of water. He was reluctant to tell her that he barely made it out alive from there too.

"When I returned to Montreal, I started getting requests from local artists to help them find buyers for their works. I realized I still had many connections from the time I worked here. At first, I was selling the works from my apartment."

"How was that?"

"Not glamorous, but it allowed me to be creative. I would take photos of the artworks and take them directly to the buyer. It meant going to places of residence, businesses, or even other galleries. Eventually, I was able to take a loan from the bank, and I started the Paradise Gallery." She had a wide smile on her face.

The waiter returned. "Are you ready to order?"

For the appetizers, Solaire ordered slices of grilled Angus beef on a bed of cannellini puree and tomatoes, while Sophie ordered grilled asparagus on a salad and potatoes with smoked cheese.

"What about you?" Sophie asked. "How did you end up in the art business?"

Solaire hated not to tell the truth, but he knew that was part of the job. Deception, secrecy, misinformation—that was what he had to do in order to protect not only himself but also those whom he was using as an "asset."

He remembered one time when he had told someone what his assignment was—this was before CIL. The consequence of this mistake wasn't as global as it would be now, but there were still repercussions, particularly for the asset. The asset was found beaten half to death by the very people Solaire was out to find information on. The asset gave up all that he knew. Solaire's life and his mission were severely compromised. He made a vow then that he would err on the side of caution, even if it meant telling a little white lie.

"I got into the art business very recently," Solaire said. "It was actually by accident. I met a man who wanted me to find something for him."

"A piece of artwork?" she asked eagerly.

"Um, yes," Solaire said. "You could say that."

Their meals came, and they dived right into them.

"Anyway," Solaire continued, "I realized I could find what he was looking for, and in return, I was paid handsomely for it." What Solaire was saying wasn't entirely untrue. Travers had shown up unexpectedly at his basement apartment in Toronto with an assignment, and Solaire was given unlimited resources to complete this assignment. "Since then, I've been traveling the globe searching for whatever my employer needs me to find."

"Sounds exciting," she said with a big smile.

"And dangerous." He quickly regretted saying that.

"How so?" she said.

Solaire thought it over. "You could say that some people will do just about anything for you to not find what you are looking for."

"Ah, I get it." There was a twinkle in her eyes. "There were others who wanted to purchase the artwork that you were interested in."

"In a manner of speaking."

"Were you always successful, or did some work slip out of your hands?"

Their desserts came. Sophie had vanilla crème brûlée while Solaire had chocolate mousse served with nougat ice cream.

"So far, I have been very fortunate," Solaire said with a mouthful of ice cream. "And I hope to continue that success here in Montreal."

"I'm glad you said that," she said. From her bag, she pulled out a catalog. It was thick and heavy. "I hope I can entice you to not leave empty-handed from the Paradise Gallery."

They went through each artwork in the catalog. Sophie, like a true saleswoman, spoke about the artist, his or her inspiration, and how this or that piece could benefit someone's collection. Solaire admired how passionate she was about her work. She truly believed in her artists and their work.

Toward the end of the catalog, he said, "What's that?"

"I'm glad you asked," she said, as if saving the best for last. The painting was of a family having a meal at the dinner table. The family was drawn lifelike while the background was entirely made up of geometric shapes. This resulted in a stunning contrast between the art in the foreground and the art in the background. One was in exquisite detail while the other was sparse.

Solaire found himself drawn to it. "I've seen something similar… outside in Old Montreal."

"Yes, you have. The artist goes by the name of Jenko," she said. "His graffiti artwork is splattered throughout the city. What makes his story interesting is that no one knows who or what he looks like. This has put his art in high demand." Sophie leaned in.

"But I'll tell you something. I'm the only one who has sold any of his artwork."

"Is that right?"

She had a huge smile on her face. "Yes, and tomorrow night I'm selling this one."

"What's tomorrow night?" Solaire asked.

"Oh, I'm sorry, I didn't tell you," she said. "I'm having my spring auction and display. You're welcome to come. In fact, you *have* to come."

"I'd love to. Maybe I'll bid on this piece by Jenko."

"I doubt you'll be able to win."

"Why is that?"

"I have a buyer who's more than eager to acquire this piece."

"Who?"

"Julian Barthez."

Solaire's eyebrows shot up. "How interesting."

"Yes. He's a huge fan of Jenko's. I've sold him one piece already, and I know he's coming to purchase this one tomorrow night."

"Why doesn't he just purchase it privately from you?"

"I offered it to him as he's been a great client of the gallery, but he insisted on bidding on it like everyone else. I think he feels it will show his support for the arts."

"What if someone outbids him?" Solaire asked.

"Do you know he's worth millions? I can't see anyone matching his offer."

Solaire paused. "I guess you're right," he finally said. He picked up his glass and raised it to her. "To great success tomorrow."

She raised hers. "Great success."

The waiter came with the bill.

She got up. "Thank you for dinner."

"You're leaving?" he said.

"I have a lot of work to do for the auction."

"Yes, but that's not until tomorrow. We still have tonight."

She looked at him. "What do you have planned, Mr. Solaire?"

"I can think of something." He had a devilish smile.

***

A man covered in silver paint, with dark sunglasses and a cowboy hat, was singing and playing his guitar.

The song was in French, but Solaire was still able to pick up some of the lyrics.

Occasional passersby dropped coins and bills in the man's guitar case.

Solaire watched him from a distance.

He was sitting at a patio of a bistro, sipping his black coffee.

It was mid-morning, and the streets were slowly becoming occupied with people.

A man approached his table and then sat across from him.

"How was dinner last night?" Levack asked with a twinkle in his eyes.

"I thought everything was on a need-to-know basis with you people," Solaire shot back.

"Okay, okay." Levack put his hands up. He waved the waiter over and ordered green tea.

"You're not going to order anything else?" Solaire asked.

"Nah, I gotta start watching my weight."

"When did this happen?"

"Since I started working with you. These missions aren't getting any simpler, you know. I feel like one day, I won't be able to outrun the bad guys because I'll be out of shape."

"I'm surprised you have managed to survive this long," Solaire said, slowly sipping his tea.

"Funny, ha ha," Levack said. "If I remember correctly, *I've* saved your behind many times now. If I were you, I'd be nice to me."

"True. And I thank you."

When Levack's cup of tea arrived, he said, "Ah, screw it. I'm hungry." He ordered a lemon danish. "So why did you call me here?"

"I've been invited to an auction at an art gallery."

"Oh, no." Levack shook his head. "If you want me to tag along to one of your fancy *soirees*, as the French like to call them, then you're out of luck, buddy. I don't do parties."

Solaire gave him a look. "I would never dare ask you on a treacherous mission like that."

"Okay, good." Levack seemed relieved. "I just wanted to make sure we are on the same page." His pastry arrived, and he dug right into it.

"At this party—which you will not be attending—I am told that Julian Barthez will also be there."

"Really?" Levack's eyebrows shot up.

"Yes, and before I go there, I would like to get some information on him."

"Why don't you do an internet search?"

"I did, and nothing relevant popped up."

"Then what do you have in mind?"

"So far, we have not been able to locate CTS, right?" Solaire said.

Levack nodded with a full mouth.

"We don't need to."

Levack stopped chewing.

"Instead, we need to go to Barthez's place of residence."

"His home?"

"Yes."

"When?"

"Today."

"Why didn't you say we would be doing physical labor?" Levack quickly waved over the waiter and ordered another danish.

***

The walls were eight feet high, and they surrounded the entire house.

There was a gate in the front with CCTV cameras.

Solaire and Levack were sitting in a Toyota Corolla Hybrid.

"Now that's what we call security," Levack said. "Only thing missing are guard dogs."

Solaire didn't reply. He was in deep thought.

Levack pulled out his weapon. "I know a way we could get in."

"No guns." Solaire shook his head.

"What's with you and guns?" Levack said. "For a guy who does what he does, you sure don't take precautions."

"Guns are dangerous," Solaire replied.

"What *we* do is dangerous."

"I don't like guns." Solaire turned to him.

"Is it a preference?"

Solaire thought for a moment. "You could say that."

"I guess we all have things that we don't like." Levack put the weapon away. "Personally, I don't like chopsticks."

Solaire looked at him.

Levack shrugged. "They're dangerous."

"And what you carry isn't?"

Levack raised his finger. "Hey, listen. If I shoot someone, chances are they are going to die. But with chopsticks, you stick those things in someone, chances are you'll only hurt them but not kill 'em. I can deal with death, but I can't deal with pain. Plus, those things hurt like hell when someone stabs you."

"I'm assuming you're speaking from experience."

"I won't confirm or deny it." Levack rubbed his right thigh. "What do we do next?"

"We'll have to come back another time."

Solaire had put the car in gear when he spotted the front gates beginning to open.

They waited, but nothing came out.

The gates then retracted and were about to close shut when they abruptly stopped.

Both Solaire and Levack looked at each other.

From their vantage point, they could see there was enough space between the gates for someone to pass through.

"I say we go for it," Levack said.

"It could be a trap," Solaire said.

"Yes, or it could be that the gates are faulty."

"I don't know."

"Well, I'm not waiting to find out." Levack got out.

Solaire reluctantly followed.

They slowly approached the front, all the while keeping an eye out. They felt as if they would be ambushed at any time.

When they were at the gates, they heard a crackle.

Levack nearly leaped in the air.

A voice sounded, and they realized it was coming from the intercom. "Welcome, gentlemen," the voice said.

Solaire looked over at Levack.

"Don't worry," the voice continued. "No harm will come to you. Please proceed up to the house."

Slowly, they entered.

They passed a circular water fountain and made their way up to the house.

The exterior was painted in white, with rectangular windows and columns going from the ground to the top.

From a distance, the house resembled the White House in Washington, DC.

A man came out through the front doors.

He walked purposefully toward them with his hands clasped behind his back.

He had a smile on his face.

"My name is Fabian Barthez," he said. "But I assume you already know that."

Solaire was about to provide the name Jim Bind, but Barthez held up his hand to stop him.

"I know who you are, Mr. Roman Solaire," Barthez said. "And you must be Mr. Donald Levack."

A look of horror spread across Levack's face.

"I make it my business to know who is following me. Oh, how rude of me. It's so uncivilized to have a decent conversation standing outside. Please come in."

Solaire and Levack hesitated until a man came up behind them.

"Don't worry," Barthez said. "Marcel is harmless."

Marcel said nothing. He merely stared at them.

The sheer size of the man unnerved Solaire.

"Please." Barthez smiled, waving his arm to invite them.

They entered.

***

The room they were taken to did, in fact, resemble the Oval Office.

It had circular walls with windows all around. One window, in particular, was larger than the others, and it faced the back lawn.

A large desk was placed before this window.

In the middle were two sofas facing each other, with a coffee table in between.

"Please have a seat," Barthez said.

They sat.

Solaire assumed Barthez would plant himself behind the large desk, but instead, he sat in a single chair, which Marcel had pulled up for him.

"Can I offer you, gentlemen, a drink?" Barthez said, crossing his legs.

"I'm fine," Solaire said.

"No, thanks," Levack said.

"You're wondering how I know about you," Barthez said.

"It crossed our minds," Solaire said.

"I'll tell you." Barthez smiled. "I have something that allows me access to certain information."

"The application," Solaire said in a matter-of-fact tone.

"Yes, and I am aware as to how you came to know about it."

"Pierre Gauthier, your former employee."

"It was unfortunate," Barthez said, "what happened to him."

"I suppose you had nothing to do with it?" Solaire said.

"How could I?" Barthez merely shrugged. "I was never near his home. In fact, I was miles away in a conference with Marcel. But I don't need to tell you that. The police reports have it all in detail. I believe they also have that Mr. Gauthier died of natural causes. I'm sure you are not here to accuse me of murder. So, why are you here?"

"How did you know we were following you?" Solaire asked.

"I saw how you gained access to CTS. Clever."

"It *was* CTS and not Digital Logistics Incorporated."

Barthez looked surprised. "You didn't know?"

"I wasn't certain."

"Ah, I see. This means our security measures have been effective."

"Not quite. I did gain access to the premises."

"True, but you found nothing." Barthez was grinning. "You see, Mr. Solaire, most companies spend a fortune deterring people from entering a location. What they fail to realize is that even a *single* breach could jeopardize their entire operation. The key is not to worry about getting in but to worry about what they may or may not find once they do. Did you find anything of importance at CTS?"

Solaire said nothing.

"I'll take your silence as a no. This also explains why you are here on my premises. But I will say that your *invasion*—let's call it that—into CTS told me that I was being targeted. I then made sure to heighten my security. When I noticed you outside my home, I decided to let you make your approach."

"Now that we are here," Solaire said, "are you going to hurt us?"

"Absolutely not." Barthez laughed. "If I wanted to harm you, there are many other ways than inviting you inside my home. I merely wanted to see who or what I'm dealing with. Now I know I have nothing to worry about."

"We know you are secretly storing data when you have told your clients that you are not."

"I am?" Barthez said innocently.

"Yes."

"Then where is it?" Barthez waved his hands around the house. "Would you like to search for it? Better yet, why don't you get a search warrant? Oh, wait… you're not the police. Who are you, really?"

"We're your worst nightmare, buddy," Levack said.

Solaire gave him a look.

Levack shrugged as if to say, *It just came out.*

Barthez said, "I have your names but nothing more than that."

"You don't have access to *everything*," Solaire said.

"Not yet, at least. But in due time, I will." Barthez glanced at his watch. "I'm sorry, gentlemen. I have another engagement later tonight."

"The auction at the Paradise Gallery," Solaire said.

"You are aware?" Barthez said, taken aback.

"Yes, I will be there as well."

Barthez didn't look amused by that.

"And I have my eye on a piece. I believe it's by an artist named Jenko."

Barthez's face slightly reddened.

"I am also interested in that piece," Barthez fumed.

"Then may the highest bidder win, I guess."

"Indeed," Barthez finally said.

Solaire and Levack got up.

"May we leave?" Solaire said.

"You were never my prisoners," Barthez said. "You were free to go any time."

"Thank you," Solaire said.

They were at the door when Barthez said, "If I were you, I wouldn't poke my nose into something that doesn't concern you. It can be deadly."

Outside, as they were rushing to their car, Levack said, "You aren't really going to bid on that painting, are you?"

"Why not?" Solaire said.

"How can you afford it?"

"I can't, but our employers can."

***

Solaire's first visit was to a men's boutique shop in Old Montreal.

He picked out an ultra-slim-fit, two-button suit. While he selected his accessories, the tailor quickly made minor alterations to the suit.

Solaire left the boutique with the suit, along with a light blue shirt, gray striped tie, and black dress shoes.

Solaire's next stop was to a car rental dealer.

He selected a black Mercedes, model SLK 360. The two-door compact roadster had a retractable roof and a Formula-One-inspired front design.

Solaire returned to his suite and then showered and shaved.

As he was putting on his shirt, there was a knock at the door.

Solaire answered.

A man wearing the hotel's uniform stood with a package in his hand.

"I wasn't expecting anything," Solaire said.

"It was addressed to you, Monsieur," the man said.

Solaire had a feeling he knew what it was. "Do you mind waiting one minute?" he said.

Solaire took the package to the bedroom and then opened it.

As expected, inside was a six-shot silver pistol.

Solaire stuffed the gun back inside the box, sealed it, and then returned to the front door.

"I need you to do something," Solaire said, holding both the package and a fifty-dollar note in front of the man.

"Anything, Monsieur." The man's eyes were fixed on the bill.

"There are some very sensitive items in this package. I need you to destroy them. Is that possible?"

"Of course," the man said, eager to please. "The hotel has *the* best disposal machine."

"Then please make certain that it is disposed of." Solaire handed both the package and the money to the man.

"*Merci beaucoup*, Monsieur."

Solaire retreated to the bedroom and then proceeded to put on his tie and suit jacket.

There was another knock at the door.

Solaire answered. It was Levack.

"Can I come in?" he said.

Solaire held the door for him.

"Travers knew you wouldn't accept the package," Levack said. "Instead, he sent me."

"I'll be fine," Solaire said.

"Remember London?"

Solaire went silent.

"Travers doesn't want that happening again."

"It sounds like he actually cares."

"It seems like it, or else I wouldn't be here."

Levack planted himself on the sofa.

Solaire went into the kitchen and poured himself a glass of water.

Solaire said, "The auction is by invitation only. Are you sure you don't want me to talk to Sophie to get you in?"

"Nah." Levack shook his head. "Like I said, I'd only cramp your style. Plus, I'd stick out in these high-brow fancy parties. I'm more of a nitty-gritty kind of guy. I prefer to stay in the shadows."

Solaire made a face. "I'll assume you'll be hiding behind the curtains?"

Levack laughed. "Wow, another joke. You're beginning to grow a sense of humor—a tiny one at that." Levack got on his feet. "No, I'll be outside, watching all the entrances and exits. Plus, I've got this." Levack held out a pen. "It has a microphone on it. I picked it up from a spy shop. I'm excited to try it."

Solaire reluctantly took the pen. "I feel like I'm in some movie."

"One day, you just might be." Levack winked.

***

The line to enter the Paradise Gallery wasn't long.

Solaire was in the Mercedes.

Up ahead, he could see cars stopping at the entrance. The occupants of the vehicles would depart, and an attendant would park the car in a parking lot a block away.

For a small gallery exhibit, it seemed like everyone in town had shown up.

As Solaire approached, reporters with cameras snapped away at his car, hoping to catch someone famous.

They stopped snapping when he got out of his vehicle.

None of them recognized him, which was exactly how he wanted it.

One reporter asked him who he was in French.

Solaire smiled and replied, "*Un visiteur.*"

A man at the door asked for his name, checked him off a list, and then held the door for him.

Inside, soft classical music was playing on the speakers.

Solaire noticed that the gallery was already half-full.

He spotted a table and approached.

Wine glasses filled with a variety of wines were neatly lined on the table.

The woman behind the table said, "*Le meilleur vin de Montreal.*" Solaire understood that she said they were the best wines in Montreal.

"Do you have anything else?" Solaire asked. "Perhaps something light?"

The woman smiled and replied in English, "We have ginger ale."

"That will do. Thank you."

The woman disappeared and returned with a wine glass filled with the carbonated drink.

"We have snacks over there." She pointed to another table. "And our auction guide is on that table."

Solaire thanked her and moved away.

The guide was the size of a small booklet. Inside there were photos of each artwork along with short bios of the artists. At the bottom were the starting prices of the bids.

Solaire flipped and flipped until he found what he was looking for.

*Diner de Famille* by Jenko was the last piece to be auctioned. The bio was only one line, stating that Jenko was an up-and-coming artist whose works could be seen throughout Montreal. The starting bid price was five thousand dollars.

"Is that too high?" he heard a woman ask him from behind.

It was Sophie, and she looked radiant.

Solaire had to stop his jaw from dropping.

She wore a strapless white dress that went down to her knees. She also wore pearl earrings with a matching pearl necklace around her neck.

"In your experience, do you think the asking price is too high?" she repeated, eager to get his input.

Solaire had to remind himself that he was representing Travers Private Art Collections. "Um… for an unknown, I would say so."

"I thought the same thing, but Mr. Barthez insisted I inflate the price."

"Why would he want that?"

"He knows he can afford it, and by raising the price, this will deter other bidders."

"He *really* wants this piece, doesn't he?"

"He told me this personally, so I'm hoping the price would be high." She almost squealed with joy. "The money would go a long way for the gallery. We mostly get local artists whose works don't fetch much, and I usually lower my commission if I know the artists could use the money, so to have this piece in our catalog will do great things for us. Why do you think all these people are here? They only came for Jenko and Mr. Barthez."

"Well, I can't speak for them, but I came just for *you*."

She blushed and then kissed him on the cheek. She moved to greet another guest.

***

There was a commotion. Solaire turned to see Julian Barthez walk through the front doors.

People rushed toward him.

Barthez smiled and shook everyone's hands.

The media had once dubbed him the boy genius for his work in Silicon Valley. Now he was the savior of the Montreal art world.

Solaire noticed that Barthez was alone, with Marcel nowhere to be found.

This either meant that Marcel didn't accompany Barthez or that he was outside somewhere.

Solaire felt his inside jacket pocket for the pen Levack had given him.

Levack was sitting in the Corolla a block away. At the first sign of danger, he would rush in.

Solaire had never cared for such precautions, but with each mission for CIL, the risks had become more and more serious.

Barthez made his way around the room toward him.

"And this is Mr. Roman Solaire," Sophie said, introducing him.

"We've met," Barthez replied with a smile.

"You have?" Sophie was surprised.

"Yes, just this morning." Barthez seemed pleased to see him.

This unnerved Solaire, but he controlled himself and said, "Yes, and I told Mr. Barthez here that I am a fan of Jenko as well."

"Indeed," Barthez said, sipping his wine.

Sophie clapped her hands in excitement. "This will be great."

Barthez leaned closer and, almost in a whisper, said, "I had plans for the painting, but now I may let you have it."

"That's very generous of you," Solaire said.

"But you *will* have to outbid me, Mr. Solaire."

"I intend to."

***

There were chairs set up in a room adjacent to the gallery.

A lectern was placed at the front where Sophie now stood.

She beamed proudly and then spoke in French into a microphone.

She spent the next several minutes talking about herself, the gallery, and then each and every one of the artists whose paintings were up for sale.

There was a round of applause when she asked all the artists in attendance to stand up.

She then introduced a man who was affiliated with a local auction house.

The man stood behind the lectern and began introducing each piece of artwork.

Assistants wearing white gloves held the pieces for the audience to see.

On several occasions, bidders requested to see the artwork up close, which compelled the assistants to walk down the aisles and display it closer for them.

Solaire glanced over the catalog. There were many items to be sold, and the piece he was interested in would be sold last.

An hour went by before one of the assistants finally brought out Jenko's *Diner de Famille*.

Sophie went over to the man behind the lectern and whispered something in his ear.

The man turned to the microphone and said, "I have been informed that we have guests who speak English, so I will conduct this bidding in English."

Solaire knew it was for him.

The man introduced the painting and then said, "Can I have five thousand?"

A hand shot up. It was Barthez.

"Five thousand five hundred?"

Solaire put his hand up.

"Six thousand?"

Barthez put his hand up.

"Six thousand five hundred."

Solaire's hand went up.

"Seven thousand?"

Barthez bid.

"Seven thousand five hundred?"

Solaire countered.

"Eight thousand?"

"I'll pay ten thousand," a voice boomed from the back.

Everyone turned.

An older man wearing a tuxedo and glasses sat with his hand up. Beside him was a tall young blonde. She smiled at him.

"Okay," the auctioneer said. "Can I have ten thousand five hundred?"

"Eleven thousand," Barthez said.

"Twelve thousand," the older man said.

Solaire watched them go back and forth until the price hit seventeen thousand.

"Can I get seventeen thousand five hundred?" the auctioneer asked.

The blonde nudged the older man, who shook his head tersely. The blonde crossed her arms and pouted.

"The price is at seventeen thousand. Can I get seventeen thousand five hundred?" The man looked around, but no one raised their hands. The price had become too steep for their tastes.

Solaire looked over at Barthez, who was staring directly at him. He had a smile on his face.

"If there are no more bids, then *Diner de Famille* is sold for—"

"Twenty thousand," Solaire said.

Everyone in the room looked in his direction.

"I'm sorry, Monsieur?" The auctioneer looked confused.

"I'll buy it for twenty thousand dollars, but not a penny more," Solaire said.

The man looked around the room. "I have to ask… will someone pay twenty thousand five hundred?"

The room was silent. The regular bidders kept both their heads and hands down.

"In that case, *Diner de Famille* is sold for twenty thousand dollars to the gentleman over there."

The man slammed the hammer down.

***

Solaire was shocked and amazed that he had just paid twenty thousand dollars for a painting.

People congratulated him and shook his hand.

Sophie rushed over and hugged him.

"*Merci* and thank you," she said.

"My pleasure." He managed a smile.

Barthez came over.

"Well done, Mr. Solaire," he said. "I never took you much for an art connoisseur, but bravo. The best man won."

"Thank you," Solaire said.

"Goodbye, and I hope after tonight, we never meet again."

Julian Barthez departed.

Solaire waited until the end. He wrote a check to the gallery when an assistant came over with the painting.

It was wrapped in bubble wrap.

Sophie handed him a small bottle.

"What is this?" Solaire said.

"The painting came with instructions. It said to spray this on the canvas after it was sold. I believe the liquid will coat the paint so that it doesn't oxidize."

"All right," Solaire said, taking it.

"Thank you." Sophie hugged him again.

***

Solaire returned to his suite with the painting in his hands.

He placed it on the coffee table and then went to the bathroom. He pulled off his jacket and tie and hung them on a hook.

He returned to the painting. He unwrapped it and examined it carefully.

Solaire knew he had purchased it to push Barthez to the edge, to see what he would do when he couldn't get what he wanted.

Instead, Barthez quit at the end. Why? Solaire was not sure.

He pulled out the small bottle Sophie had given him.

The liquid was clear, and when Solaire sniffed, it was odorless.

He gently sprayed it on the canvas. He then placed the painting on the sofa.

He went to the bathroom and pulled off his shirt. He turned the tap on and let the water fill the tub.

He put his fingers underneath the tap to check on the temperature when he smelled something.

It was bitter and pungent.

He went out and sniffed.

It was now strong and overwhelming.

He sniffed some more until he realized it was coming from the painting.

He got closer and took a whiff.

Suddenly, his eyes started burning.

He jerked back in agony.

His throat constricted, feeling like it was on fire.

He felt a sharp pain in his chest. He had trouble breathing.

His right arm went numb.

The room swirled around him. He was instantly dizzy and nauseous.

Solaire tried searching for the phone but couldn't remember where it was.

He fell into the bathroom.

He pulled himself up to the sink. He was now choking. He put two fingers down his throat and vomited hard.

He was sweating profusely.

He felt as if a heavy object was placed on his chest. The pain was intense and blinding.

He tried to scream, but only a weak moan came out.

He fell into the tub, which was now filled with water.

The coldness hit him hard and strong.

Water went into his nose, mouth, and ears.

He tried lifting himself out, but he no longer had any control over his limbs.

He felt helpless as the tap filled the tub with water.

The last thought Roman Solaire had was that he was going to drown.

***

His eyes snapped open.

It was dark.

He blinked once and then twice.

He was in a room.

He searched and spotted a man standing near the windows.

It was Travers.

Before he could say anything, he fell asleep.

He woke up to find light streaming through the windows.

He looked around.

He was in the same room, but this time he recognized that he was in a hospital.

Everything looked and smelled sterile.

Solaire tried to get up, but his entire body felt like lead.

He tried swallowing but felt pin pricks down his throat.

He was hooked up to wires that went into monitors and other devices.

The door slowly opened, and in came Levack.

"Hey there, buddy," he said with a smile. "How you doing?"

"Surviving," Solaire managed to say.

"Yeah, we almost lost you there."

"Where am I?"

"Montreal General Hospital."

"What happened?" Solaire asked.

"You were poisoned."

"Poisoned?"

"Yep, doctors said you're lucky to be alive."

"How did I get here?"

"You know the pen I gave you?"

Solaire nodded.

"Lucky for you, I forgot to turn it off. I heard you were in distress, so I rushed in. I found you in the bathtub, nearly submerged. In fact, the doctors said had you not been in the water, you would have surely died. The water cleared out most of the toxins before they got to you. Good thinking."

"I wasn't. I fell in."

"Oh. Then good job falling in."

"Thanks," Solaire said.

"For what?"

"For saving my life *again*."

"Nah, don't mention it. You're my meal ticket, buddy."

Solaire looked at him.

"If you're not around, then I got no job."

"I remember seeing Travers in the room."

"He was here all night. He arranged for this private room."

"I thought I was dispensable."

"We all are, but I think he may have a soft spot for you."

"Or maybe he needs me to keep doing his dirty work."

"You gotta cut him some slack. In my years, I've seen a lot of good agents left to dry. Travers may be secretive—he has to be in our line of work—but he takes care of those who work under him. Heck, he got me watching your back. And if I hadn't shown up at your suite, who knows what could have happened."

Solaire understood. "I'll go thank Travers later. First, we need to find Sophie. She may be behind what happened to me."

"Okay, you want me to go talk to her?"

"No, I want to do it myself."

"Are you sure about that? Last I checked, you nearly died."

"I'm fine. I have to finish this now."

***

She was in the gallery, examining one of the paintings when they walked in.

She smiled, but it quickly faded when she saw the look on his face.

"Are you okay?" she said.

"Can we talk?" Solaire asked. "Privately."

She looked at her assistant and then at Levack, who was standing near the doors. "Sure," she replied.

She took him to her office in the back.

"What's wrong?" she asked once they were alone.

"How do you know Julian Barthez?" Solaire asked.

"He's a customer," she replied. "He regularly comes to the gallery to buy paintings."

"And nothing else?"

"No, nothing," she said.

"Don't lie to me." Solaire's voice was hard.

"Why would I?" She looked scared and confused. "Why are you asking me this?"

"Last night, the painting I bought at the auction was covered with a toxic chemical. That chemical was activated by the spray you gave me to put on the painting. I nearly died, Sophie."

She cupped her mouth. "Oh my god." Tears formed in her eyes. "I swear, I did not know."

"Who gave you that painting?" Solaire had to control himself from raising his voice.

"Guy Fournier. He works as a middle man between artists and galleries. He brought me Jenko's works."

"Where can I find him?"

She went behind her desk, searched, and handed him a card.

It was Fournier's business card with an address on it.

"I'm so sorry, Roman," she said. "If I had known…"

"Did he give you instructions about the spray?" Solaire said.

"Yes, and I thought it was unusual, but he said it came from Jenko. I never questioned it because Jenko is a private but remarkable artist. I was honored to have one of his works displayed at my gallery. I now wish I had…"

Solaire went silent. The hardness faded from his face.

"I'm sorry," he finally said. "But I needed to know."

"I'm sorry for what happened to you."

"I have to go." Solaire turned to leave but stopped. "The previous piece of Jenko's that you sold to Barthez… did it have the same instructions regarding the spray?"

"Yes, it did."

"Thank you."

***

Solaire sat in one of the wooden pews at the back.

He was inside Notre-Dame Basilica in Old Montreal.

The eighteenth-century church was built in a Gothic architectural design. It was both grand and colorful. The stained-glass windows depicted the religious history of Montreal, not biblical scenes found in other churches. It also had a pipe organ, which dated back to 1891.

The church was open to the public at a nominal price.

Solaire wasn't a religious man, but he did appreciate the work that went into building this magnificent place.

A man came and sat on the bench in front of him.

Solaire leaned over and whispered, "I need answers."

"About Pierre Gauthier?" Travers said.

"Yes. Why did he contact CIL?"

"He didn't contact us… *we* contacted him. We knew Barthez was involved in something dangerous; we just didn't know what. We needed someone on the side, and Gauthier became our man."

"I'm assuming he didn't line up to be CIL's informant?" Solaire said.

"No, he didn't. Barthez is a smart businessman. He pays his employees well. This enables him to buy their silence. Why would you expose your employer when he is compensating you quite handsomely? We tried on many occasions, without raising any alarms, to recruit CTS employees, but it was all futile."

"What was different with Gauthier?"

Travers went silent.

"I need to know."

Travers sighed. "Gauthier had a criminal conviction on his record. In college, he had gotten into an argument with a student, and viciously beat him up. It was during a frat party, though, and Gauthier was seriously drunk. But he was charged with aggravated assault, and he did time in prison for it. Having that mark on his record didn't help him find a job. CTS was the best job he ever had."

"But there is something else?"

"Yes, his wife. She wasn't aware of his past. We…" Travers went quiet. "We approached him and threatened to tell his wife about his time in prison. He begged us not to, and we agreed that if he helped us, we would go away."

"You blackmailed him?" Solaire's tone was hard.

"I'm not proud of it, but yes." Travers turned and faced him. "What we do is ensure that nothing happens to international stability. This means that sometimes we have to do things that may go against our beliefs, but these things are necessary for what we are trying to achieve."

"The end justifies the means?" Solaire said.

"Yes, it does."

"What about his wife and his family? Had we not been involved, he may still be alive."

"I know, and this is something I'll have to live with. But Roman, if I didn't make those difficult decisions, I don't know if I could live with myself knowing what the other outcome would be. Barthez must *not* be allowed to provide vital and secure information to dangerous regimes. If that ever happened, who knows what damage it could do."

It was Solaire's turn to go silent. He looked down at his hands. He was going through a lot of emotions, but deep down, he knew Travers was right.

"I brought what you asked for." Travers held a manila envelope.

Solaire took it.

Inside there were police photographs taken at Gauthier's house at the time of his death.

"It took some persuading, but I managed to get them."

Solaire quickly flipped through them.

"You think Gauthier was poisoned just like you?" Travers said.

"I am certain of it."

"How will the photographs prove that?"

"I don't know, but I need to see how Gauthier died."

Before Travers could say anything more, Solaire got up and left Notre-Dame Basilica.

***

He was of medium height and slightly overweight. He wore a tight turtleneck sweater, which exposed his protruding belly.

Guy Fournier was inside his studio office, talking to a pretty girl.

Solaire and Levack were sitting in the Corolla, watching him from across the street.

They got out and approached the studio.

Fournier was talking excitedly, and it looked as if the girl was interested in what he was saying.

"*Ooh, un client*," Fournier said, turning to them. "*Bienvenu.*"

"Are you Guy Fournier?" Solaire asked just to make sure.

"*Oui*, yes."

"Can we talk alone?" Solaire glanced over at the girl.

"*Nous allons discuter plus tard, Isabel*," Fournier said to the girl.

She smiled and then left the studio.

"How can I help?" Fournier asked.

"We are here about Jenko," Solaire said.

"Sorry, but I don't have any works by him," Fournier said.

"We are not here for another one of his paintings," Solaire said. "We want to meet him."

"Meet him?" Fournier looked incredulous. "*I* have not even met him."

Levack said, "Then how are you selling his work?"

"Are you the police?" Fournier eyed them suspiciously.

"No, we're not," Solaire said.

"Then I don't have to tell you anything," Fournier replied.

"Yes, you do." Levack cracked his knuckles.

"You are threatening me?" The color on Fournier's face drained.

"We just want some information," Solaire said. "How did you get Jenko's paintings?"

Fournier looked at Levack and then said, "A man gives me the paintings."

"Jenko?" Solaire said.

"I don't think so. He doesn't say much but gives me the paintings with a note."

"Do the notes have instructions?" Solaire said.

Fournier shrugged. "*Oui*."

"What kind of instructions?"

"Silly stuff, like spray painting with a bottle. Who puts water on work of art? *Ridicule*. It is stupid. Water will ruin the painting. Everyone knows that. I don't agree with it, but I have no choice."

"The man who gave you the paintings, what does he look like?" Solaire asked.

Fournier shrugged. "I don't see him too good. He meets me at night."

"Where?"

"Behind a building in a… how do you say? *Ruelle*."

"Alley."

"Yes."

Solaire pulled out a photo of Barthez. "Could it be this man?"

Fournier examined it and then shook his head. "*Non*. The man is bigger. This man is small."

Solaire pulled out a photo of Marcel. "How about him?"

Fournier eyes widened after examining it. "*Oui*, I think so."

"Tell us everything," Solaire said.

Fournier looked at them both and then sighed. "Okay, okay. One day I get a call from someone—I don't know if it is this man, but he tells me to meet him about Jenko. I was very excited. Jenko is genius. I know if I sell Jenko's painting, I can make good money. So, I go. I wait in the… alley, and a car comes up. A man get out of the car and give me the painting with the note. I ask about money, but he goes back in car and leaves. I come back to my studio and check, and it is original Jenko painting. You see his painting on the walls of buildings?"

"Yes," Solaire said. "I've seen his work around Montreal."

"I check with that to make sure. I am a hundred percent sure it is Jenko who paint it. The note also says to only sell to the Paradise Gallery."

"Why them?" Solaire asked.

"I don't know. They are a boutique gallery, but the owner, Sophie Paradis, is good for local artists. Maybe this man thinks Jenko is a local artist, so the Paradise Gallery will be good for him too."

"Do you think Sophie is somehow involved in this arrangement?" Solaire had to ask.

Fournier shook his head. "I don't think so. She looked very surprised when I bring her the paintings. She ask why I choose her, and I tell her it was Jenko's choice. I only follow instructions."

"How do you pay Jenko?" Solaire said.

Fournier shrugged. "I can't."

"What do you mean?"

"Okay, I tell you how it works. I give painting to Sophie to sell. When the painting sells, she gives me the money less her percentage for her gallery. I take my share and try to give this man. But when I do, he doesn't take the money. I still have the money. You want it? I write you a check."

"We don't care about the money," Solaire said. "It doesn't belong to us. Can you give us this man's telephone number?"

"I can't," Fournier said. "The telephone number is blocked. I answer it and he gives me instructions to when I meet him and where."

"And you have no other way of contacting him?" Solaire said.

"*Non*, I don't. I wish I could. If this man works for Jenko, then I want to give Jenko his money and meet him and thank him. Jenko is a true artist and a fellow *Quebecois*. He is an inspiration for every artist."

Solaire knew whatever Fournier knew, he had already told them. There was no point in trying to get anything more out of him.

"Thank you for your time," Solaire finally said.

***

Solaire went back to his suite, feeling tired and dejected.

So far, he had failed to find anything that would lead him to Barthez and his storage facility.

Even tracking Jenko was becoming a dead end.

How Jenko was involved with Barthez, he didn't know, either.

Solaire went into the bathroom and returned after splashing himself with cold water.

He had thought about changing suites or even to another hotel, but the thought of getting Barthez was now occupying him.

Barthez had let him outbid him at the auction. Now he knew why.

But what if Solaire hadn't shown up at Barthez's house? Was there another target?

Barthez had purchased a painting legitimately through the Paradise Gallery and then had given it to one of his employees, Pierre Gauthier, who didn't live long enough to appreciate it.

Who was he going to purchase the second painting for?

Solaire was never going to know now. He felt he had gone through all avenues and had come up empty.

Who else could he talk to? Who else could he follow that would lead him to Barthez?

Solaire shook his head and sat on the sofa.

If he were a drinking man, he would drown himself in his sorrows.

He had escaped death only to find that he was no closer to catching the man who had threatened his life.

On the other side of the living room, Jenko's *Diner de Famille* stared back at him.

He couldn't believe he had paid twenty thousand dollars for something that was meant to kill him.

Solaire shook his head.

He leaned over and grabbed the canvas.

He held the painting and examined it.

He couldn't believe that just the night before, this very painting could have been the end of him.

The top layer of the canvas now had tiny bubbles, and some areas even had what looked like corrosion.

The toxic material reacted when it made contact with the liquid in the spray bottle and released a lethal toxin.

The canvas now had remnants of the reaction.

Solaire closely looked at each detail on the painting, going from top to bottom. He stopped when he spotted something.

Underneath Jenko's signature were tiny numbers. The numbers were followed by a *W*.

A thought raced through his head.

He went to the bedroom and returned with the envelope Travers had given him.

He quickly flipped through the photos taken at Gauthier's house.

He stopped at one and looked at it closely.

The photo was of a room. A painting hung on the wall, and below it, on the floor, was a chalk mark of where Gauthier's body was found.

Solaire went to the mini-fridge. He pulled out a small bottle of liquor, poured its contents out, and returned.

He placed his eye on the mouth of the bottle and used it as a magnifying glass.

It wasn't crystal clear, but Solaire could make out numbers on the painting at Gauthier's house.

The numbers were followed by an *N*.

Solaire's brow furrowed.

He looked at the photograph again and then at Jenko's painting in his suite.

Then it hit him like a thunderbolt.

*They were coordinates.*

*N* was for north and *W* for west.

Solaire quickly reached for the phone and called Levack.

***

"Are you sure this is the right place?" Solaire asked.

Levack looked at his GPS. "It is, according to the coordinates you gave me."

"I've been here before," Solaire said.

They were in Saint-Henri, at the address Travers had given Solaire at the beginning.

"It's just an abandoned building," Solaire said, looking around. "I checked it myself."

"Then I guess we are SOL, again," Levack said.

"I'm not going back empty-handed." Solaire pulled out a flashlight. He clicked it on and then moved toward the building.

"You sure we should be going in?" Levack asked.

"Why not?" Solaire replied.

"It's getting kinda dark."

"I never took you for someone who was afraid of the dark."

"I'm not, but my mom told me never to go into deserted buildings at night."

Solaire ignored his comment and proceeded further. He pulled back the same wooden board he had gone past before and entered the building.

He probed his flashlight around and could see the dirt and debris scattered everywhere.

He felt Levack behind him.

"Nice place," Levack said. "A real fixer-upper."

Instead of staying on the ground floor, Solaire moved to the stairs.

On the second floor, he searched each room but came up empty.

"Told you there wouldn't be anything here," Levack said. "We should go."

"No!" Solaire said, a bit loudly.

Levack stared at him.

Solaire composed himself. "I'm sorry, you're right. I was hoping that—"

"Come on, buddy," Levack said, slapping him on the back. "I'll buy you an iced tea with no ice."

They were going down the stairs when Solaire suddenly stopped.

"Did you hear it?" he asked.

"Hear what?"

"A noise."

Levack listened. "I didn't hear anything."

"I know I heard it."

Levack was about to protest when he heard a cry. It was loud but muffled.

Solaire looked at him.

"No kidding." Levack's eyes were wide. "You were right."

Solaire moved around the stairs. Behind it, hidden away, was a door.

A bolt was locking it.

Levack quickly looked around and returned with a fire extinguisher. "I don't know why people leave these things behind."

He hammered the bolt, breaking the lock.

They were confronted with another set of stairs, these leading down.

Levack pulled out his gun.

Solaire aimed the flashlight, and together they went down.

They were in a small but spacious room. The walls were lined with canvases of all shapes and sizes. They spotted painting materials and even various buckets of paint.

"*Vous etes ici pour m'aider?*" a voice asked.

They instantly turned.

A man sat on a chair with his arms and legs tied to it. A partially loose piece of duct tape hung from his lips.

The man repeated the same words in French again. Solaire was able to decipher some of it.

"Yes, we are here to help you," Solaire said. "Who are you?"

"I am Jenko," the man replied in English. "Can you free me?"

Solaire removed the tape from his mouth while Levack loosened the restraints.

"Thank you," Jenko said.

Jenko was tall and slim. He had sharp features with a thin mustache and a goatee.

"Are you the police?" he asked.

"Not really," Levack answered. "But, we are international."

"What were you doing here?" Solaire asked.

"Painting," Jenko said, as if it was obvious.

"For who?"

"Monsieur Barthez."

"But why?"

"I don't know. One night I am painting on the side of a building, and then this big man comes and instructs me to get in the car. I say no, but this man looks mean, so I do. Next thing I know, I am here, forced to paint these." He pointed to several completed canvases. "I am an *artiste!*" He pounded his chest. "I am not an assembly line. I cannot create masterpieces if I am not inspired. These are rubbish."

"I paid twenty thousand dollars for your rubbish," Solaire said.

"You did?"

"At an auction."

"I don't do this for the money. This is an insult to my work."

Solaire said, "I don't want to add insult to injury, but your art is being used to kill people."

A look of horror spread across Jenko's face.

"I am afraid it's true," Solaire said. "Did you put those coordinates on the paintings?"

"Yes, I had to do something. I was lucky Monsieur Barthez didn't realize what I was doing."

"It led us to you."

"Can we leave?" Jenko said, rubbing his wrists. "I don't want to be here another minute."

On the way up the stairs, Levack asked, "What's your *real* name?"

"An artist never reveals his identity," Jenko replied back.

***

When they reached the top, they froze.

Standing before them was the menacing figure of Marcel.

Just behind him, to the side, was Barthez with his arms behind his back.

"We meet again, Mr. Solaire," Barthez hissed. "I see that you have met this city's renowned artist, Jenko."

Levack slowly reached for the gun in his pocket.

"I wouldn't do that, Mr. Levack," Barthez said. "The outcome may not be very pleasant."

"I was just going to scratch my leg."

"I'm sure you were." He nodded to Marcel, who relieved Levack of his weapon. "Now, if you follow my instructions, things will go very smoothly. If you don't, then I won't promise that no harm will come to you."

They were escorted out of the building and taken to the one next to it.

This building was in disarray like the one they had just come from.

They went down a flight of stairs and were confronted with a large steel door.

"Mr. Solaire, I believe this is what you've been searching for," Barthez said.

Marcel swung the door wide, and inside they could see rows upon rows of computer servers.

Several technicians in white lab coats turned in their direction.

"Please, go in," Barthez said, waving his hand.

The room was hot, and there was a whirring sound of machines running at full capacity.

"This is where you store the data," Solaire said.

"Very observant."

They were led down a narrow hall and then to another door.

The room wasn't large, but it was open with high ceilings.

In the corner, a figure was on the floor with their hands and feet restrained. The figure looked up at them.

It was Sophie.

Solaire instinctively moved toward her.

Marcel put his hand out, stopping him.

Sophie's mouth was shut with duct tape.

"I'm sure you remember each other," Barthez said.

One by one, their hands and feet were tied together. They were made to sit on the floor.

"Let her go," Solaire said. "Your quarrel is with me."

"Ms. Paradis was never supposed to survive this long," Barthez said.

Solaire said, "The second painting you were going to purchase. It was for her."

"Good deduction, Mr. Solaire." Barthez smiled. "I was going to give it to her as a gift for being such a strong supporter of local artists. Unfortunately, you came along and ruined it."

"But why her?" Solaire asked.

"Loose ends. After I was done with Gauthier, I would eliminate Ms. Paradis."

"What about Guy Fournier?" Solaire asked.

"Mr. Fournier would meet a different end—in a dark alley."

Jenko quickly interjected. "But you promised to let me go after I did what you asked."

"You're foolish to believe your captor after you've seen his face."

Jenko's face turned pale.

"While I admire your work and talent, I'm afraid your services are no longer required."

"You're sick," Solaire said.

"No, I'm a businessman, Mr. Solaire. My business is providing information to the highest bidder."

"But why?"

"You, Mr. Solaire, wouldn't understand what I've been through."

"Try me."

Barthez looked at him and then smirked. "All right, I'll tell you. After the dot com crash, I was cast aside like an outsider. What was my crime? I had only held on to *my* company so that I could see it grow and prosper. I wasn't the only one who had lost money. Hundreds of other companies lost millions, but I was treated worse than a murderer. I lost everything: money, status, reputation. I knocked on every door, only to have it shut in my face. So, yes, I made deals with the devil, but at the end of the day, the devil was willing to pay more. That's capitalism for you."

"No, it's selling your country to people who have ulterior agendas," Solaire said.

"Call it what you will, but it's a straightforward business. If my government had been willing to invest in my company, then maybe I wouldn't have had to look elsewhere."

"We can still work something out," Solaire said.

"It's too late now. I have agreements in place, which I have to follow. My business partners wouldn't take it so kindly if I walked away. I hope you understand."

"I do understand. You are a traitor."

"Call me what you will. After tonight your opinion will not mean anything."

***

"Are you planning on killing us?" Solaire asked.

"You've left me no choice, Mr. Solaire." Barthez nodded to Marcel.

Marcel moved toward him and, in one smooth motion, released Solaire from his restraints.

Solaire looked confused.

"There is a misunderstanding out there that Marcel is the one to be feared," Barthez said. "In actuality, it is *me* who you should be scared of."

Barthez rolled up his sleeves and moved around the room.

"You can still let us go," Solaire said, rubbing his wrists.

"Not quite. Your friends' end will be swift and painless. Yours, on the other hand, will be anything but that."

Barthez spread his feet and lifted his fists up. "I picked up a few things while I was living in Asia."

"Do you expect me to fight you?" Solaire asked.

"Yes, Mr. Solaire, I do. If you don't, then..." A smile crossed his face. "You know the outcome."

At lightning speed, Barthez took three steps and hit Solaire squarely in the chest.

The impact was so powerful that Solaire flew two feet in the air and landed hard on the concrete floor.

He clutched his chest as the pain was intense.

"Get up." Barthez circled him like a predator toying with his prey.

Levack tried to get on his feet, but Marcel pulled him down by his shoulder.

Marcel grunted his disapproval.

Solaire slowly got on his feet.

"Defend yourself," Barthez commanded.

Solaire put his fists up, but he was no match. In quick succession, Barthez hit him six times—in the stomach, chest, arm, ribs, head, and finally his face.

Blood spurted out of his mouth as he fell to the floor.

His entire body was on fire.

*Here we go again*, he thought.

"Vital points," Barthez said, caressing his knuckles. "The human body has many sensitive spots that, when pressed, can cause unimaginable pain."

"Why don't you just get it over with?" Solaire spat.

"Over? I've only just begun."

Barthez reached over to lift Solaire up when Solaire swung his right hand at him. Barthez reacted quickly and countered with a shot at Solaire's kidney.

Solaire's legs buckled, and he fell once again to the floor.

Tears flowed down his face.

"Stop it!" Levack yelled. "Why don't you pick on someone your own size?"

"How heroic of you to offer yourself, Mr. Levack," Barthez said. "But I must decline. Your punishment will be to see your friend suffer—and suffer he most surely will."

Solaire tried to get on his feet. He wanted to put up a fight. If this was how he was going to die, then he wasn't going to give Barthez any satisfaction from it.

He put his fists up again.

A smile curled across Barthez's face.

Barthez moved forward and swung his open hand at Solaire.

Solaire blocked it, but before he could attack, Barthez shot his elbow hard across Solaire's chin.

Solaire's head jerked back.

He tried to control his balance but fell to the floor.

Solaire's chin felt hot and wet.

He knew he was bleeding and badly.

Solaire made another attempt to get on his feet, but this time Barthez was on him, pinning his arms with his knees.

Barthez lifted his fist in the air.

"Goodbye, Mr. Solaire."

Solaire readied himself for the impact.

Before Barthez could bring the fist down, there was a loud commotion. Barthez looked up.

"*Police!*" a voice yelled.

From his vantage point, Solaire saw men in black riot gear storm the room.

One came over and pulled Barthez off Solaire. A pair of officers collared Marcel.

Solaire wanted to say something, but before he could, he passed out.

***

The water was clear and blue.

From high up in the balcony, Solaire could see the Saint Lawrence River in the distance.

The sun had come up not too long ago.

Solaire sat in the wheelchair, staring silently at the magnificent scenery before him.

His body was healing much quicker than expected, but the wheelchair was a precaution. His body had endured a lot of punishment, and doctors had ordered him to rest, which meant staying still.

Solaire looked around his surroundings. Travers had put him up in a condo not far from the river. Travers felt the fresh air would do him some good.

He heard a noise at the door.

He twisted.

Sophie entered the condo. *"Bonjour!"* she said with a smile.

*"Bonjour,"* he replied back.

She came out on the balcony and kissed him on the cheek.

"I brought breakfast," she said. "Strawberry crepes, Belgian waffles, assorted baguettes, eggs with black truffles, and the best coffee in the city."

"I can't eat all that," Solaire said.

"You're lucky." She smiled. "I'll help you."

She went back inside when there was a knock at the door.

Travers came in and made his way to the balcony.

He took a seat across from Solaire.

"How are you feeling, Roman?" he asked.

"Better. Much better."

"It seems that whenever we meet, you are either searching for information or you are in some sort of trouble."

"I guess that's one way to define our relationship. What happened to Barthez?" Solaire asked.

"Julian Barthez is in our custody, and he will be charged for selling information to countries that do not have our best interests in mind."

"How did you find us? I mean, in Saint-Henri?"

"After what happened to you with the painting, I wasn't going to take any risks," Travers said. "I tracked the GPS on Levack's Corolla. When I saw that it had stayed in one location for too long, I knew something was wrong. I contacted my friends at the Montreal Police Services, and we raided the location. It took some time to find where you were in those buildings, but I am glad to say we made it just in time."

Solaire looked away.

"Thank you," Solaire finally said.

"For what?" Travers asked.

"For saving my life *twice*. Once with the painting, and then with Barthez."

"Don't thank me. If it weren't for you, we wouldn't have been able to locate Barthez's data storage facility. You led us there."

"Thank you anyway."

Travers leaned closer. "If you think I only care about the mission, then you would be very wrong for thinking that. Roman, you are more vital to the Court of International Law than you would believe. Even if they don't know what you have done for them, I do, so I should be the one thanking you."

Solaire stared at him.

Travers got up and extended his hand.

Solaire shook it.

"Get some rest," Travers said. "Our international fight with criminals is just beginning."

He left.

Sophie came over with a tray filled with their breakfast.

They spent the next half-hour devouring everything before them.

They laughed and joked and teased one another.

At one point, Sophie looked at Solaire and then kissed him.

"Gratitude?" he asked, smiling.

Sophie giggled. "*Oui*."

Solaire kissed her back.

There was another knock at the door.

Sophie answered.

"Can you give us a moment?" a familiar voice asked Sophie.

"Certainly," she replied.

Levack came over and gave Solaire a big hug.

Pain shot through him, but he still managed a smile.

"How is my favorite spy today?" Levack said.

"I don't know if I would call myself a spy," Solaire said.

"If you don't, then I will. What I've seen you do in New York, London, and now here in Montreal… that, my friend, is what I call spy work."

Solaire said, "What are you going to do now?"

"Go home to Cleveland," Levack said.

Solaire waited, knowing full well that Levack wouldn't say much more than that. But this time, he was wrong.

"I've got a wife and two children waiting for me. My son is in high school, and my daughter will be starting high school soon. I've been happily married to the same woman for almost fifteen years now," Levack said with pride.

"Congratulations," Solaire said.

"Thank you. I can't say it's all due to me. I don't know what she sees in me, considering I'm mostly away, but I love her with all my heart."

"She's a lucky woman to have you as her husband. I'm lucky to have you as my friend." Solaire put his hand out.

"Aw, don't make me cry now. I'm a big softy inside. Ah, the hell with it." He leaned over and gave Solaire another hug. "I hope your lady friend didn't see that." Levack winked. "She may begin to wonder about the peculiarities of our complex and covert relationship."

"I'm sure she'll understand." Solaire smiled back.

Levack got up. "You know I have to ask… will I see you in another city?"

"You bet your life, you will," Solaire replied. "But first, I'm going home to Toronto and taking a very long vacation."

Visit the author's website:
**www.finchambooks.com**

Contact:
**finchambooks@gmail.com**

Join my Facebook page:
**https://www.facebook.com/finchambooks/**

THOMAS FINCHAM holds a graduate degree in Economics. His travels throughout the world have given him an appreciation for other cultures and beliefs. He has lived in Africa, Asia, and North America. An avid reader of mysteries and thrillers, he decided to give writing a try. Several novels later, he can honestly say he has found his calling. He is married and lives in a hundred-year-old house. He is the author of the Lee Callaway Series, the Echo Rose Series, the Martin Rhodes Series, and the Hyder Ali Series.